EXECUTIVE ORDER
AN ALEX MASON THRILLER

DAVID ARCHER

BLAKE BANNER

RIGHTHOUSE

ISBN-13: 978-1-63696-307-5

ISBN-10: 1-63696-307-2

Cover design by: Damonza

Printed in the United States of America

www.righthouse.com

www.instagram.com/righthousebooks

www.facebook.com/righthousebooks

twitter.com/righthousebooks

PRAISE FOR ALEX MASON

ALEX MASON THRILLERS
Odin (Book 1)
Ice Cold Spy (Book 2)
Mason's Law (Book 3)
Assets and Liabilities (Book 4)
Russian Roulette (Book 5)
Executive Order (Book 6)
Dead Man Talking (Book 7)
All The King's Men (Book 8)
Flashpoint (Book 9)
Brotherhood of the Goat (Book 10)
Dead Hot (Book 11)
Blood on Megiddo (Book 12)
Son of Hell (Book 13)

ONE

I DROPPED THE NEWSPAPER ON THE SEAT NEXT TO me as the train came to a halt at Union Station, in Washington DC. There was a brief scream of tortured steel that echoed under the vaulted ceilings above, a jolt and then a big sigh as the train seemed to deflate and the doors hissed open.

I stood, grabbed my leather bag and made for the exit where a group of passengers had become logjammed. I paused to wait and somebody collided with me from behind. I turned and an attractive young woman smiled at me. "I'm so sorry," she said, "I wasn't looking where I was going."

Her eyes were an intense green, which with her strawberry-blonde hair made her face startling. She had a Cupid's bow mouth and a smile you wanted to keep talking to. I smiled back and stood aside. "Please, after you. I am not in a hurry."

She gave a shy nod, slipped past me, dodged through the logjam and, through the train window, I watched her trot away through the crowds. By the time I eventually stepped out onto the platform she was gone from view and had largely slipped from my mind. I found a cab and told the driver, "The Commonwealth Tower on Wilson Boulevard, across the river."

The drive was uneventful, along Constitution Avenue and over the Theodore Roosevelt Bridge, where the Potomac moved heavy and slow, rich with broken early morning light. We negotiated Spaghetti Junction and pretty soon we pulled up outside the Commonwealth Tower. I paid him the fare and reached in my jacket pocket for some coins to make up the tip, and that was when I found the neatly folded piece of paper.

I walked into Nero's office in the 1I section of the ODIN maze on the top floor of the tower, frowning at the piece of paper. The door closed behind me with a soft hiss and I continued to frown at it. After a moment Nero's voice intruded on my thoughts and I looked up.

"Have you arrived yet, or is it just your body that has walked through the door?"

I held up the piece of paper. "A list."

"Are you being deliberately cryptic in the hope of annoying me?"

"No." I sat. "It's a list of names. A couple are familiar, others I don't know. It's a photocopy of an original."

I slid it across the desk. For a moment he ignored it and simply watched me with what you could only describe as baleful eyes. Then he reached for the list and looked at it.

"Helen Troy," he said, reading the name at the top of the list. "The candidate for nomination?"

He glanced at me and I shrugged. "I have no idea. I found it in my pocket when I paid the cab downstairs. I don't think Helen Troy is a common name, so it is likely to be her."

He grunted softly. "You'd think most people with the surname Troy would have the good taste not to call their daughter Helen." He studied the list a moment longer. "Frank Costello and James Reed are also candidates for nomination in the same party. Recent leaks about Costello's ties with the Mafia have damaged him less than expected." He glared at me under an arched brow, like it was my fault. "Robert de Niro and Al Pacino seduced the American public into a love affair with the Mafia that endures to this day." He looked back at the list. "The clear favorite is James Reed, however. We still prefer our leaders to be from Anglo-Saxon or Irish stock. Troy lags behind the other two. Why is her name underscored?"

He sank back in his chair, inhaled deeply through his nose and held the piece of paper as though it were Yorick's skull.

"The first three are candidates for nomination. The next, Paul Hirschfield, is not an uncommon name. There is a Paul Hirschfield attached to the Israeli Embassy. He is a colonel in the Mossad. Israel has let it be known, quietly, that they favor Reed because his stance on Islam and Israel is unambiguous, whereas Troy and Costello are more wishy-washy. Priti Anand could refer to the American-born Indian financier. The Anands are billionaires and she has established herself as one of the richest, and most powerful women in America. And Johannes de Jong, born in South Africa, became a dotcom billionaire at twenty-one. Now, since the stock market crash you failed to stop this spring, he owns controlling shares in AI Incorporated, Cyber-Solutions and Tex-Oil."

He looked over the piece of paper at me and I smiled sweetly.

"My shoulder still hurts when the wind blows from the east."

"What, aside from this piece of paper, connects these people?"

"The first three are members of the same party, the last two are prominent financial backers of that same party, and Colonel Hirschfield supports that party quite vocally because that party supports Israel. So the party connects all the people on the list."

"Correct, but there must be more. I shall make discreet inquiries as to which of the candidates Anand and de Jong plan to back." He pressed a buzzer on his desk. When Lovelock's lovely voice oozed, "Yes, sir?" he snapped, "Come!"

The door opened and she entered, looking as lovely as she sounded. He handed her the list. "Copy this to the Archive and get them to send me everything they have on these people. Have them send it to Analysis too, and tell the spotty fellow," he waved his fingers at his head, "the one with greasy, unwashed hair—"

"Graham—"

"Graham, have him and Navneet analyze it. I want to know what has caused these names to be present together on this list."

"Yes sir."

She gave me an immoral wink and left on immoral legs.

Nero watched the door close and mused, "Navneet. It makes you wonder, what conjunction of social forces drives a parent to name his son 'Fresh Butter.' They could have called him Ravi, God of the Sun, they could have called him Pranav, Sacred Syllable, or even Son of Lord Buddha, Rahul. But no," he shook his head, "they called him Fresh Butter."

"Sir?"

He shifted his eyes to meet mine. "Think, how did you come by this list?"

"I think it was slipped to me when I was getting off the train at Union Station."

"Reason?"

"A young woman collided with me from behind. She was sweet and pretty and hurried on ahead of me."

"That is your reasoning?"

"That, and the fact that nobody else got that close to me from when I left Gallin at the hotel in New York until I arrived in DC."

"Gallin..." He drummed his fat fingers on the desk. "It is too much of a coincidence that she is a katsa and there is a Mossad intelligence officer on that list, and you are slipped the list returning from seeing Captain Gallin. But what does it mean? None of these others are connected to the Mossad, as far as I know."

"She's still in New York, you want me to talk to her?"

"No. I don't want you to talk to anyone until we know more. I am troubled also by the fact that Helen Troy's name is underscored twice, making her some kind of priority. Whoever wrote this list wrote her name and then wanted to express, 'Especially her,' or 'First her,' 'In particular *her!*'"

"You're thinking it's a hit list."

He pursed his lips and nodded, then gave a "maybe" shrug. "It could be." He flapped a hand at me. "Very well.

Go and see Senator Troy. Telephone Captain Gallin and ask her if she has any idea why the colonel's name should appear thus on a list with members and supporters of this party. Please mention no other names. See what she has to say."

"Yes sir." I went to stand but hesitated a moment. "You wanted to see me about something, sir. That's why I came back from New York..." I tried not to sound resentful.

He made an affirmative grunt. "Your friends who planted the suitcase bomb[1], and whom you allowed to get away, they have surfaced in Brazil."

"I was injured, sir, and it seemed to me that confirming that the nuclear device was deactivated was more..."

"Never mind," he interrupted me. "The information the CIA have is that they both died in a car crash near Belem. Dental records and fingerprints confirm it is them, though the bodies were burned beyond recognition."

"Oh." I nodded. "Rough justice."

He gazed at me a moment. "You're sentimental at heart, Alex. It's your only real weakness. That and a lazy mind." He drummed his fingers on the desk a moment, then went on. "It seemed a little convenient to me, so I had our operative inquire a little deeper and he confirmed they were alive and well living in Belize as Mr. and Mrs. Sedgemore. Discreet inquiries at the CIA and in Russia reveal that both are satisfied Peter and Maria are dead[2]."

"But..."

"Naturally it was my duty to consider requesting that Cobra review their case for possible crimes against humanity."

"Cobra?"

"Never mind. An agency you don't need to know about.

But in the end I concluded that our operative must have been mistaken, and I have closed the file on them. I trust you approve."

"I do, sir. I don't believe in epiphanies, but these two were the exception that confirmed the rule. They could have made billions by allowing the bomb to explode, but they defused it. I think that calls for a second chance."

He gave me a long level look, then said in a flat, dead voice, "And besides, they are dead."

"And that, too."

"Go and see Ms Troy. Sound her out, don't mention the list. See if any of the names mean anything to her. Talk to your friend, Captain Gallin. No names. Leave."

I left but paused on my way out to get Helen Troy's address from Lovelock and ask her, "Why do people make lists, Lovelock?"

She arched a devastating eyebrow at me. "Is this a 'women love shopping' question? You should know I self-identify as a woman who does not like shopping." I sighed and made for the door. She stopped me with, "I once made a list of men I might be unfaithful to my husband for."

I paused and looked back at her. She was smiling and winked.

"You weren't on it, honey. There was only one name on it, Sean Connery, but he was already in his seventies."

"Mish Moneypenny," I said, arching an eyebrow of my own, "shay it ain't show."

I rode the elevator down to the parking garage to collect my Factory Five Mk4 Roadster. I lowered the hood and rumbled out into the early summer sunshine still thinking about lists. It struck me that people made lists for just three reasons. In all three cases it was to have a precise collection of data handy, either A) to refer to it in some task like writing a book or putting together a piece of furniture, B) to be able to pass that data on, as in teaching a class, or C) to be able to eliminate those data from your list, as in a to-do list, a shopping list, or a hit list.

I told Siri to call Gallin. She was as cheerful as ever and made the call.

"So soon, already? You know there is nothing less attractive than a needy guy, Mason. Except maybe a drunk guy with sleep apnea."

"Are you done?"

"I just don't want you to ruin what could be a beautiful friendship."

"Now are you done?"

"Jeez! Get on with it! What do you want?"

"Why would Colonel Paul Hirschfield be on a list?"

"What kind of list?"

"A list I am instructed not to share with you, but which holds candidates for nomination, all in the same party, a couple of billionaires who are known to back that party, and the colonel."

"I need in."

"One step at a time, Sweet Aila. Does it make any sense to you that he is on that list?"

She didn't answer for a moment, then said, "What? No. I'll call you back. Wait. Where did you get hold of this list?"

"That's the trouble with this relationship, see? I give, give, give, and you always hold back."

She sighed as I turned onto the George Washington Memorial Parkway and started to cruise comfortably beside the river. "OK," she said, "no, Alex, on the face of it I cannot think of any particular reason why Paul should be on a list, except that several hundred million people would probably like to assassinate him. So, unless you give me more data, I can't help you."

"Being married to you would be a nightmare."

"I agree. Now, unless you are going to give me more data I am going to call my dad so he can call your boss and make you give me more."

"Fine."

She hung up as I left the Three Sisters behind me and was enveloped by trees. Fifteen minutes later my phone rang. It was Nero.

"Alex—"

"Yes, sir."

"I have just had the head of the London field office of the Mossad on the telephone to me."

"Yes, sir, Gabriel Gallin."

"Quite so. Good man. We've been friends for many years. Master chess player. Superb palate."

"Yes, sir. And Captain Gallin's father."

"Indeed. He feels the business of the list may have security implications for Israel. Colonel Hirschfield may be a target."

"Yes, sir. We had pretty much come to that conclusion ourselves, hadn't we? But do I gather you have changed your mind about briefing Captain Gallin?"

"No. I never change my mind, Alex. I have simply reassessed the facts. She'll be joining you here in DC. Read her in."

"Yes, sir."

He hung up.

It was a delightful drive up to Great Falls. There were more trees than people, which is always a good sign. Also, it was one of those places where the creatures who had inflicted the Great Hive of the grid system on the American people lived, happily and comfortably, among random, asymmetrical lanes and drives which adapted organically to the homes they served, creating a natural, spontaneous beauty, rather than defining the cubicles in which "the people" had to live in order to derive the greatest efficiency from their existence. Here the streets were not A, B, C or 1, 2 and 3. Here people lived on River Bend Road and Cornwell Farm Drive, and Little Piddle Lane. And as I weaved and wended my dappled way toward Jackson Lane, I felt certain nobody here would ever commit an impolite crime, and whatever crimes they did commit, they would never be so vulgar as to get caught.

Helen Troy's mansion was a vast jumble of neo-Victorian gables, turrets and faux-leaded windows that only needed a little lightning to be cast in an Addams Family movie. It was set among sweeping, well-behaved lawns against a backdrop of abundant trees that would not have been out of place in Vermont. There was, sadly, no twelve-foot wall and no iron gate guarded by ravens, and no lightning or thunder as I parked outside the door. There was however, a small distance away, outside the double garage, a small Toyota and the big Jaguar which was being washed by a huge black guy with his sleeves rolled up over arms like tree trunks.

I climbed from my Roadster and crossed the well-behaved lawn to ring on the doorbell. It was not opened by a hunchback with one eye, but by a pretty, South American maid in a pretty blue uniform with a white apron. Privilege will bring you these mundane pleasures.

"Good morning," she said, smiling like she really believed it was one. "Can I help you?"

"Yes," I told her. "I need to talk to Ms. Troy."

"You have an appointment, Mr...?"

"I don't need one," I said pleasantly. "Mr. Mason, Alex Mason. You could tell her I am here from the Office of the Director of Intelligence Networks."

I showed her my card and she nodded at it, then ushered me in and showed me to the office.

"Please, wait here. I will tell her."

The office looked like she'd taken a photograph of the Oval Office and tried to recreate it in her home. Maybe she had. The carpet was blue, the desk was walnut and set in front of three tall windows, there were two cream sofas perpendicular to the desk and there was even a portrait of Benjamin Franklin on the right as you looked at it.

After a couple of minutes the door opened and the woman who had been causing so much talk and speculation in the media was standing looking at me. She was in a pair of Levis that looked very happy to be where they were. She had on a plaid shirt with the sleeves rolled up and she was holding a wooden spoon with cake mix on it.

"Who are you," she said, "and what do you want?"

TWO

AT ABOUT THE TIME GALLIN HUNG UP ON ME TO tell her dad to talk to my boss, Colonel Paul Hirschfield was organizing his pens in the walnut penholder his wife—his *ex*-wife—had given him for his fifty-eighth birthday. Red pens on the left, blue pens on the right. He smiled and shook his head sadly in a way only Jewish people know how to do, and considered the recent American practice of making Republicans red and Democrats blue. All his life the reds had been the Commies, the bad guys. Now the reds were the Republicans. You just didn't know who to trust anymore.

Recent! He snorted softly to himself. Twenty years ago! They had started referring to "red states" and "blue states" more than twenty years ago! Time. Time must be a woman because she was the greatest and most subtle traitor of all! He nodded and smiled. He liked that. He made a note, using a blue pen on a small notepad he had started carrying around with him since he'd decided to write his memoirs. He'd like people to remember him not just as a right-wing hawk, but also a man with a sensitive, poetic streak. And wit! Wit was important.

He put the pen back and called his wife. His ex-wife. She answered on the third ring.

"What? I told you not to call me. I spoke to Ira and he told me you shouldn't call. I could get a court order, you know that? I should do that. I should get a court order to stop you calling me every day. What do you want?"

"How are the kids?"

"That's what you called me for? To know how the kids are!"

"I miss them, they're my kids too. Do they miss me?"

"They're grown up, Paul. That's how they are. And they visit you twice a week. It's a shame you didn't miss them so much when they were kids. This whole thing might have been different."

"You think so?" She didn't answer. "What about Saul?"

"He has a cold, he's droopy. He's lying on the sofa now watching the old cartoons."

"Which ones?"

"Bugs Bunny, and the Road Runner. Remember...?"

She trailed off but he didn't notice and spoke over her. "I love Bugs Bunny and the Road Runner. We used to watch them together, remember? We'd cuddle on the sofa with Saul between us. And laugh! I never get tired of them."

"He misses you."

"Rub Vicks into his feet. Then you put woolly socks on his feet and cover him on the sofa with a duvet. Give him ginger and honey."

"I know how to treat a cold, Paul."

"I miss him."

"He misses you too."

"How about you?" But he didn't give her time to answer and asked, "You seeing a lot of Ira?"

"Paul, don't start that again. He's our lawyer! I'm not seeing anybody! What about you? With your balls and dinners and all your fancy friends!"

"You know I don't attend those functions. I work. And when I'm not working, I work. I go home to my empty house, and I work."

"I remember." It was only partly a criticism. "If only you hadn't worked so much."

"Time," he said and sighed, about to unveil his newly crafted phrase, but thought better of it, lest it be taken as a veiled recrimination, and instead crafted a new one: "It makes us all wise, but always too late."

"You always had a way with words."

"I'll be retiring soon."

"Maybe you could come for lunch, Sunday. Today's Friday. That would be the day after tomorrow."

"I know when Sunday is. Will Ira be there?"

"No, for heaven's sake!"

"That would be nice. I miss you, Ruth."

"I know."

"Not just the kids."

"I know."

"Us, you, me, the kids. The family. It's not right."

"I know. You have to stop now. Come for lunch."

She hung up and he sat and wept for a few minutes in silence. When he had stilled the spasms of grief in his belly he dried his eyes with his neatly folded handkerchief, collected his briefcase and stepped out of his office and into his secretary's office. She looked up at him and he paused in front of her desk.

"I have some things to attend to, Alice. I'll have my phone switched off for a couple of hours. After that you can find me at home." He was about to leave but hesitated a moment, then smiled. "Except Sunday. Sunday I'll be having lunch with my wife."

Alice grinned. "Oh, Colonel, is that a good sign?"

"It may be, Alice, wish me luck."

Colonel Hirschfield took the elevator down to the parking garage, collected his nondescript 2019 Honda Accord and emerged onto International Drive NW. Despite the deep relationship between Israel and the United States, and the deep reliance the two nations had on each other, the Israeli Embassy was not with the other major embassies along the river on Reservoir Road, like the French and the Germans, or ostentatiously on Massachusetts Avenue, like the British. It was discretely tucked away up beside Soapstone Valley, along with the Embassies of Ethiopia, Pakistan and Bangladesh. Some friends you received in the back room or the kitchen, others you were seen out with at the opera or in fancy restaurants. It's what diplomacy is all about.

He made his way along Van Ness and south down Connecticut Avenue, and eventually found his way to the Target shopping mall on 14th Street in Colombia Heights. There he bought a burner phone and took a walk. It was a VoicePing P-one Android cell phone for seniors, otherwise known as a Dumb Phone. What he liked best about it was that it did not have a touchscreen. While he walked he lamented the stupidity of the new age, and dialed a number he'd memorized; a number at the White House. It was answered immediately.

"Who is this and how did you get this number?"

"Jerry! Is that a way to greet an old friend?"

"Jesus, Paul! What the hell are you playing at? You can't —! And what's this number?"

He spoke fast, in a low voice, and Paul could visualize him moving quickly away from any people he had nearby.

"What's the matter, Jerry? You become suddenly anti-Semitic? You don't want people to know you're talking to Israeli Intelligence?"

"Come on, cut it out! What do you want, Paul?"

"I want to talk to my old friend, Jerry, security advisor to the president, who did such a superb job on the recent suit-case bomb crisis."

He spoke as though through clenched teeth. "I told you that is going to take time."

Paul sighed. He had reached Park Road and turned left toward 16th Street. "See, here's the thing, Jerry. I don't have a lot of time. Time is like patience," he said, telling himself he had come up with another nice line about time, "the more you use it, the less you have of it. And that applies to you and me both, Jerry."

"*I just haven't got that kind of money available right now!*" His voice was a savage whisper.

The colonel crossed Hyatt Place at the pedestrian cross-ing, carefully checking in both directions before stepping onto the blacktop.

"That's OK," he said. "I have to admit that my conscience has been causing me trouble. I am basically a good man with good values. But I am tired! I feel I am getting old, you know? So I thought it would be a good idea to secure an early retirement with a million bucks in the bank—"

"You said five hundred grand!"

"I know, but that's the way it goes, you see? Now you've said you're not going to pay, so I am free to fantasize! What's the difference? You're not going to pay anyway, right?" He laughed. "But in any case, like I was saying, it's a relief anyway because my conscience was troubling me. I should not let a bastard like you get away. At least, if I pass my information on to the CIA, their Special Activities Department will know what to do with you."

"No, now slow down, Paul! I didn't say I wouldn't pay!"

"You disgust me, Jerry. How many people died in Silicon Valley? Five thousand people? Women, children, old, young, killed in the most horrific way. And how much were you paid to facilitate that?"

"Paul, please—"

"No, you're right. I would rather look at my face in the morning knowing I had reported you, than look at my bank account knowing you were free."

"All right! All right!"

"I am going to have a nice weekend with my family, Jerry. And Monday morning, my first order of business when I sit down at my desk, will be to call the director of the CIA."

"Paul! Stop! This very afternoon you will have your five hundred grand—"

"One million bucks, Jerry. And if you procrastinate again it will be one and a half. Do it today. I'll check my account when I get home." He hung up and smiled, and muttered quietly to himself, "And then I'll call the CIA, you spineless traitor."

He removed the SIM card from the cell as he made his way back toward the shopping mall. As he walked he folded it in half a few times until it tore, dropped one piece in a trash can and dropped the other down a drain. The phone he slipped in his pocket, intending to incinerate it in the furnace in his basement of his house.

At home on Warren Street NW he left his car out front in the shade of the plane tree and made his way up two flights of stone steps to his redbrick porch, counting them as he had twice every day for the past ten years: seven in the first flight, seven in the second. And, as he had done twice a day for the past ten years, he joked to himself, "Still all there."

He closed the door on the bright sunshine and inhaled the cool, shady peace of his hallway. Six months ago the silence had startled and depressed him every time he got home. Now he had grown used to it and told himself it was one of the few things about being single he would miss if Ruth ever came back to him. The blessed silence.

He made his way to the drawing room and opened the French doors onto the backyard, where three steps led down to his patio. There was a patch of sun at the end by the red roses that made the green stand out, vibrant. He could smell the sweetness of the roses on the air. He went inside and mixed himself a Beefeater and tonic, with plenty of ice and lemon, and as he was about to descend the steps to his patio, his old-fashioned house phone rang. He gave God a baleful look, shook his head and sat on the sofa by the phone.

"Hello, this is Colonel Paul Hirschfield speaking."

The voice on the other end, pretty and feminine,

laughed. "Paul, do you seriously always answer the phone like that?"

"Oh," he said without much enthusiasm, "hello. Yes, I do. There was nothing wrong with it when my parents taught me to do it, and there's nothing wrong with it now."

"You're a rare treasure. Listen, Paul, have you thought about what we talked about?"

"No, I have thought about what you talked about, and I am afraid my answer is the same as it was then—"

She interrupted him. "Paul, you don't realize how important this is for me. It could swing everything. All I need is a word in his ear. He listens to you, he respects you—"

It was Paul's turn to interrupt. "Everyone in Washington listens to me and respects me. You listen to me and respect me. You know why? Because I have integrity. Because I give good advice. Because I am honest. And what you are asking me to do, Minnie, is dishonest."

"It's not dishonest! It's just..."

She trailed off and he said, "And *that's* dishonest. Telling yourself a thing is not dishonest when you know damn well it is. You're trying to walk a tightrope, Minnie, and it can't be walked. You want to court Arab oil and Jewish bankers, and you are going to end up getting badly hurt. If I go to Ben and tell him, I think you should endorse what Minnie is trying to do, I will lose all my credibility and all his trust. Because what you want to do does not benefit Israel, and it sure as hell does not benefit the United States."

"I've always thought of you as an uncle, Paul, one of the family. You know that."

"And I have always tried to teach you the values my

parents taught me when I was a kid. I know it hasn't been easy for you without your parents' guidance, but you have to hold fast to the righteous path."

"I'm sorry, Paul. I shouldn't have asked."

"Forget it. It's this town. Everybody is crazy for power. But my father, God rest him, drummed it into me every day of my childhood: 'Paul,' he'd say, 'power at any price is not power at all. It's slavery!'"

"I know, Paul, he was a wise man."

"OK, Minnie. We should get together soon. It's been too long. You've been busy, I've been busy. But you should come for lunch. Not this weekend 'cause I'm going over to Ruth's for lunch!"

"No kidding! Is this a sign of things to come?"

"Oh, I hope so, kiddo. I miss 'em so much, I can't tell you."

"I bet you do. Hell! *I* miss her and I'm not even married to her!"

"Yeah, I know, everybody loves her. Trouble is, she's tired of me. And that is one thing you can't do anything about."

"Give her time. She might come around. I think she still loves you, Paul."

He saw his hand shaking and fought to control his voice. "No, she feels sorry for me. But she's with Ira now. It's over, and to tell you the truth, Minnie, I'm about ready to move on."

"You got anyone in mind, you old dawg?"

"No, but I'm looking, and that's a good sign, right?"

They both laughed, promised to stay in touch and get together soon and he hung up.

He sat for a long time staring at the blank TV screen opposite. Eventually he blinked and realized he was still holding his gin and tonic. He placed it untouched on the lamp table beside the sofa and stood. He made his way up the stairs, crossed the broad landing and went into the matrimonial bedroom. He opened the top drawer in his nightstand and extracted a Sig Sauer Tacops P226, rammed in a magazine and went downstairs again. There he half closed the drapes, sat in the armchair in the corner of the room, beside the French doors, pulled over his gin and tonic and drained half of it.

He laid the semi-automatic on his lap and stared at it for a long while. When he looked at his drink again the ice cubes had all but melted. He drained what was left, closed his eyes and tried to steady his nerves. He had killed more than once in his life, on active duty. This would be just the same...just the same. Just point the gun in the right direction and pull the trigger.

THREE

I GAVE MYSELF A SECOND TO ASSIMILATE HER. SHE was charismatic without trying. There was an intensity to her that was magnetic. I took my time smiling and told her, "My name is Alex Mason, I am with the Office of the Director of Intelligence Networks at the Pentagon."

"You got some ID?"

I showed her my card and she said, "What do you want?"

I took the card back and held her eye for a moment. "I am also a voter," I said, "so you might try being polite."

"How about you tell me why you're in my house, Mr. Mason? And I'll decide whether to be polite."

"I'm in your house because your maid let me in. You want me out, all you have to do is say so. I was at your door, ringing on the bell, because your name appeared on a list, and we were concerned for your safety. As far as I am aware, that is not a violation of your constitutional rights."

"That's enough, Mr. Mason. I have a right to know why there is an intelligence officer in my house. What is this list?"

"What it is, is confidential, Ms. Troy. Now how about I ask you some questions, you answer them if you want to, and if you don't you don't, and then I leave?" I could see from her eyes and the set of her jaw that she was about to tell me to go to hell, so I preempted her. "Ms. Troy, like I said, I am here because we are concerned for your safety. You have a family. We are concerned for their safety too. I am having trouble understanding why that makes you mad."

She cleared her throat, bit her lip and folded herself onto one of the two cream sofas, with a politician's smile glued to her face.

"Go ahead, ask your questions."

"Do I have to ask them standing up? Only, when I publish my memoirs and *Time* magazine interview me, I'd like to tell them how polite you were when I met you."

She gestured to the sofa opposite and I sat.

"We have come by a list with several names on it. I can't tell you how we came by the list, but I can tell you that your name was at the top, underscored twice. Of those names three, including yours, were of candidates for nomination by your party, two more were prominent supporters of your party, and one was an intelligence officer for a foreign government. Does such a list mean anything to you?"

She stared at my face for a moment without expression, then turned the same expressionless gaze on her desk.

"No," she said at last. "It means nothing to me." She turned her gaze back to study my face again. "I can guess at the two candidates, they are obvious. But as to the backers and the intelligence officer..." She shrugged. "Was it an Arab?"

"No. The list may be perfectly harmless, but the way we

came by it suggests somebody wanted us to know the list existed."

"Why?"

"So what we need to establish as a matter of urgency, is whether this is a hit list."

Her eyes went wide. "You think somebody wants to assassinate me? I'm just an also ran! Frank and Jimmy are far more likely to win the nomination than I am!"

I was shaking my head. When she'd finished I said, "I didn't say that. I said we need to establish *whether* it is." I gestured at her with my open palm. "You have kind of answered my next question. Can you think of anyone who might want to put you on a hit list? Clearly, on the face of it, you can't. But I would ask you to give it some thought anyway. You are charismatic, you are popular, you are garnering a lot of support from male and female voters. Maybe you are treading on somebody's toes."

Her eyes went back to the desk. "I'll give it some thought."

"Have you got any kind of private security? A bodyguard...?"

"Not as such. I have my driver. I haven't felt it was necessary until now."

"We can arrange that for you if you like, or you can arrange it yourself. Either way, I would recommend it."

"All right."

"And Ms. Troy?"

She frowned at my tone. "Yes?"

"Let *them* advise *you* on how to run your security."

Her face acquired all the warmth of a January morning in Reykjavik. "Is there anything else, Mr. Mason?"

I nodded. "Are you married?"

"How is that any of your concern?"

"Because your husband may have a more objective view of any threats you face, or any enemies you might have." She bridled and I went on. "Not because he is more objective, or because he is a man, but simply because he is not you."

"My husband died seven years ago. So you'll have to settle for my female subjectivity."

"No, I won't." I smiled. "You must have a secretary or a PA."

"I have a personal assistant. She takes care of most things for me."

"May I speak to her?"

She stood and walked to her desk where she pressed a button and said, "Dolly, come to my office, would you?" Then she rested her ass on the edge of the desk and watched me. She still had the wooden spoon in her hand. "I hope this is not going to become too intrusive, Mr. Mason."

"And I hope you're not going to get shot, Ms. Troy. But if I have to get intrusive to make sure you don't get shot, you can be sure I will become very damn intrusive. Do I have to apologize for that?"

There was a tap at the door. It opened and Dolly stepped through. She stared fixedly at me for all of three seconds, then blinked. She was young and attractive, her eyes were an intense green which, with her strawberry-blonde hair, made her face startling. To cap it all, she had a Cupid's bow mouth that made you want to stop and talk to her. I smiled and said, "Hello."

She swallowed hard, said, "Good morning," and turned to her boss. "Yes, Ms. Troy?"

"Mr. Mason has some questions for you."

"Yes, Mr. Mason, how can I help you?"

Her eyes were pleading with me not to mention the train. My eyes told her to relax.

"How long have you been working for Senator Troy, Dolly?"

"Two years last March."

"I want you to think real hard now. Can you think of anyone at all who might want to cause Senator Troy harm, to the point of perhaps ordering a hit on her?"

"Heavens, no!"

"You know, Dolly, I find that answer hard to believe. All politicians, especially those with promising careers, have enemies."

She stiffened and squared her shoulders. "Obviously she has competitors who might try to discredit her, if that were possible, but to the point of ordering a *hit!* I just can't believe that."

"OK, so who do you think would want to discredit her?"

She glanced at her boss with those startling green eyes. "Well, Mr. Frank Costello and Mr. James Reed are both seeking nomination against Ms. Troy, and both are steadily losing ground to her."

"Anyone else?"

"No." She shook her head.

"I may need to talk to you again, Ms...."

"Scott, Dolores Scott."

Helen Troy cut in, "I'll give you her number when you leave. That will be all, Dolly."

"Yes, Ms. Troy, Mr. Mason." She gave a little bow and left.

"I bet she's efficient."

"Very."

"But a little naïve for your game."

"My game?"

"Politics."

"Looks can be deceiving. Was there anything else, Mr. Mason?"

"Not for now, Ms. Troy."

I stood. She wrote down a number on a pad and tore off the page, then crossed the floor and opened the door for me. "Next time, Mr. Mason, please telephone and make an appointment first."

I stopped in the doorway and looked down at her. She had that kind of metal in her eyes you get from learning at an early age that you have to face the world alone, and win.

"Then there would be no surprise," I said.

She handed me Dolly's number. "Good bye, Mr. Mason."

I smiled. "I'll be sure and tell *Time* magazine you were real sweet."

I let myself out the front door and eased myself behind the wheel of the Mk4. I sat a while, drumming my fingers on the steering wheel, knowing they were both watching me. As I pulled out of the drive and headed south back toward town, I called Lovelock.

"What do you need, lover boy," she oozed into my ear.

"Aside from you, slightly moist from the swimming pool, I need the address of Dolores Scott, personal assistant to Helen Troy."

"Give me five minutes."

I hung up and my phone rang.

"Hello Aila—"

"Meet me at Ronald Reagan Airport."

"You're flying?"

"No, I'm going by bus. I just like airports so I want you to meet me at the airport."

"The way you drive it would be quicker by car."

"I'll be landing in half an hour."

"You're phoning from the plane?"

"No, this is telepathy and I just made you *believe* it's a phone call. Jeez, Mason! What's today, Obvious Day?"

"You're not supposed to use your phone on the plane, Aila."

"Yeah, kind of crazy, anarchic chick I am. Go to the airport, Mason, and wait for me there. Do *not* go and see Paul without me. Understood?"

"Mm-hmm. Paul, huh? You two close?"

"He's a good man."

"OK."

I took a leisurely drive to the airport and sat staring at a double espresso while I waited for her to show up. She appeared eventually in an enormous pair of black sunglasses and a flimsy cotton dress that insinuated everything and said nothing. When she saw me she slid the shades onto her head, grinned, said, "Hey tiger," and feinted a couple of hooks to my floating ribs.

"You're a strange woman, Aila."

"Oh Lord, he's calling me Aila. Can an indecent proposal be far away?" I ignored her, picked up her bag and started toward the parking lot. "Just because we visited in New York, doesn't mean you have to call me Aila. You don't want to marry me, do you? It would be OK, only the sex would be embarrassing. Tell me about this list."

I watched her with narrowed eyes while I dumped her bag in my trunk. She smiled brightly and got in the passenger seat.

"OK," I told her as we took the exit north toward Washington. "When I was getting off the train this morning at Union Station, coming back from visiting you in New York, Helen Troy's personal assistant pretended to collide with me and put this list into my pocket." I handed her the photocopy of the list. "That is a photocopy, obviously, but the one she handed me was also a photocopy. That's a photocopy of the photocopy."

I kept quiet while she examined the list. After a moment she screwed up her brow.

"Helen Troy's PA?"

"Yeah, I showed the list to Nero and he told me to go see her—Troy, not her assistant."

"So at that point you didn't know..."

She fingered her hair from her face and I shook my head. "At that point I didn't know who the girl was who bumped into me. But when I went to see Troy, she called in her PA and bimba!"

"Bimba? What are you, Italian?"

"There she was, the girl from the train."

"So did you do a big reveal?" She pointed vaguely through the windshield. "Take Wisconsin."

"Do I look amateur? I retained an unflappable demeanor and secured her telephone number and her address. But something struck me forcefully. They were both concealing something."

"Were they both concealing the same thing, or each something different?"

"I don't know. And I'll tell you something else. I am unsettled by Colonel Hirschfield's name on that list." She grunted agreement and I asked her, "You want to go see him first?"

She nodded. "Yeah, he has a ton of experience and lots of contacts. If he's on a list he'll have some idea why. He will orientate us and we'll see where we go from there."

"Orientate?"

"Yes, Mason, orient is a place, orientate is a verb, just as alternate is odd-even, yes-no, on-off whereas *alternative* is another option."

"You going to tell me how to spell color next, Aila?"

"Stop calling me that."

She pulled out her phone and made a call. After a moment she said, "Colonel Paul Hirschfield, please." She listened for a moment, then said, "Oh, OK, thank you." She hung up and turned to me. "He's at home."

"You know where he lives?"

"Yeah." I waited and she added, "So, what can we nail down and say for sure about this list? About what it means?"

I nodded. "It's purpose is either as a data bank for reference or communication, or it's a hit list—"

"OK, and it is political, specifically about this party—"

I nodded some more. "And I would go a step further and say it is about the future president, because everyone on the list has something invested in the future president: Troy, Costello and Reed have money, time and ambition invested,

Anand and de Jong will invest money if they haven't already, the odd one out is the colonel."

She grunted, "Do we know who Anand and de Jong are planning to back?"

"Nero is making discreet inquiries. You think that's relevant?"

"It could be. You don't?"

"It doesn't make me snap my fingers and go, *Aha!* They're all on the same list. If it was about competition between the candidates, one candidate should be missing. Then who the backers were backing would be relevant if the missing candidate was the one they were *not* backing. Does that make sense?"

"For some reason it does. So it's about politics, it's about the next president, it's..." She trailed off, then asked, "Is it about Israel?"

"For now let's just say it's about the colonel. It's about politics, it's about the next president, it's about Colonel Paul Hirschfield and it is something Dolores Scott wanted me to know about."

At McDonald's she said, "Take 39th, then right into Warren."

It was about halfway down on the right. There was a pretty nondescript Honda Accord parked outside in the shade of a large plane tree. I killed the engine and we both looked at the house for a moment. It seemed very quiet and still.

"He recently got divorced," she said absently, as though that might explain the stillness and the quiet.

"You know a lot about this guy. How close are you?"

She smiled and chuckled but didn't look at me. She climbed out of the car and I followed her up two flights of seven stone steps through the front yard to the porch. She rang on the bell and we waited. I peered through the front window but there was nothing to see except a dining table and a dresser. She rang two more times, then said, "I'm going in."

FOUR

"Before you shoot the lock or kick the door down, you think maybe we should try the backyard?" I pointed to the end of the porch. There was a small gate and some steps. "We can get there from here."

We moved down the side of the house among bushes and lawn that had been neglected and were beginning to show it, to a seven-foot redbrick wall with an arched, iron gate in it. The gate was padlocked.

"Now can I shoot it and kick it down?"

"No." I pulled my Swiss Army knife from my pocket and selected the screwdriver, which I hammered into the lock with the heel of my hand and opened the padlock. I pushed the gate open and she went through. I closed the gate behind us and asked her in a soft whisper, "That's a real pretty dress. Where have you got your weapon?"

She ignored me and we came to a large, unkempt lawn fringed with trees and a flight of four broad steps that led up to a patio at the back of the house. There were sliding

French doors which stood partly open, and the drapes partly closed. By contrast with the bright sun outside, the room looked dark.

I climbed the steps and she sprinted up ahead of me, stepping to the side of the plate glass. I followed suit, pulled my P226 from under my arm and slid the door all the way open. Nothing happened. I glanced at Gallin behind me and frowned. She had a Sig in her hands. She winked at me and I stepped into the living room with the weapon held out in front of me. There was nothing and nobody immediately visible.

In my peripheral vision, on my right, I was aware of a fireplace and a TV. On my left there was only deep shadow. Barely a second had passed and I turned, aiming the gun into the shadows.

I froze. There was a man sitting in an armchair. His right arm was hanging down, with his fingers trailing on the floor beside a Sig Sauer Tacops. His head had flopped onto his right shoulder and he had a large hole in the left side of his head. The wall was spattered with gore.

Gallin was looking up at me from the patio, a few inches away, with the sun in her eyes. She knew from my expression. I said:

"We're too late." I hesitated. "How close were you, Gallin? We can have somebody from the embassy identify him if you prefer."

She shook her head. "Not that close, Mason." She stepped past me and looked down at him. "That's Paul," she said. "Is this a suicide?"

I called the office. After a moment Lovelock put me through to Nero.

"Report!"

"We have a situation, sir."

"Of course we have a situation! Everything is a situation, dammit! Be precise!"

I scowled at the phone. "We have just arrived at Colonel Paul Hirschfield's house. He was not answering the door so we entered via the backyard, his French doors were open..."

"Get to the point, Alex!"

"He appears to have committed suicide in his living room."

"How?"

"Shot himself in the right temple."

"Nobody shoots themselves in the temple. It is practically impossible."

"I know. We don't want the cops walking all over this, sir. You need to talk to the embassy, inform the MPD that we have jurisdiction. And we want our forensic team here an hour ago."

"I will arrange it, but if the Israeli Embassy owns that house technically they have jurisdiction. I'll get back to you. Meanwhile, look but do not touch."

I hung up and hunkered down, looking at the entry wound and the exit wound.

"How old was he?"

"I don't know, late fifties."

"He looks tough. He saw active duty?"

"Of course. And plenty of it."

"So he's done his Krav Maga."

"Obviously."

"So he is not going to just sit there quietly while some

guy puts a gun in his hand and makes him blow his own brains out."

"No way. He would have attacked while they were giving him instructions."

I pointed at his head. "But the trajectory of the bullet, Gallin, it's perfect, through and through, in the right temple and out the left. That's almost impossible to do. There is always an involuntary jerk of the hand at the moment of firing. Typically the bullet grazes the skull diagonally, or it goes in the temple and out the crown."

"What's your point?"

I shook my head. "I haven't got one right now, except that this is contradictory. I don't believe he could have fired that shot."

"But it's just as hard to believe anybody else did."

I sighed and stood, studying the blood spatter. There was no question it was his. It was seamlessly on his shoulder, on the chair and on the wall, and looking closely I could see the slug embedded in the plaster.

Gallin pointed to the empty glass on the lamp table. "Glass, no bottle," she said. "You would have expected a person building up to suicide to drink a bottle of scotch, not have one gin and tonic."

She crossed the room and stood looking at the dead man. Eventually she said, "Do I believe it?" After a deep breath she said, "Almost. He was devoted to his family. I mean, seriously. He was crazy about his wife. And his kids..." She shook her head. "When his wife left him he just went to pieces."

"Why'd she leave him?"

"I don't know. I only met him once, in Tel Aviv at a

conference. But we got on well and he'd tell you his whole life story in ten minutes. He was a bit of a legend at the Academy, too. Everybody knew him. He adored his family. It may have been too much for him." She took another deep breath. "Did he have that kind of control where he could shoot himself through the head? If half what they say about him is true, maybe. What is impossible—more impossible than that shot—is that he allowed this to be done to him."

I gave a soft grunt. Outside I could hear vehicles pulling up. "We'll have to wait and see what the forensic team says." As I went for the door I spoke over my shoulder. "We should go and inform his wife. Maybe find out why she left him."

I opened the door and the ODIN forensics team filed in with their equipment, trying and failing to be discreet. They stopped in the hall and started putting on their space suits. Ted was the team leader. He had a blond beard and pale blue eyes through which he smiled as we shook hands.

"Ted, he's in the living room at the back. The initial problem we have is that the shot is too good to be self-inflicted, but there is no sign of a struggle. This guy is a colonel in the Israeli army, lots of combat experience, Krav Maga—"

"Got it."

"Slug's in the wall."

"We need to go over the whole house with a microscope. Copy of the report to me, one to the director, one to the Israeli Embassy and one to Captain Gallin care of the embassy. And we need to expedite this, Ted."

"You got it."

"Mason." I turned. She showed me her phone. Some-body was calling her. "It's the embassy. I'm going to take this." She waved her finger around, taking in the house. "If this is Israeli territory, everything, *everything*, goes through me. Yes sir?" She listened, then looked at me and nodded. After a moment she said, again, "Yes sir," and hung up. "This house belongs to the Israeli Embassy and is technically part of Israel. We have agreed to a cooperative investigation with ODIN, but I lead and everything goes through me. Understood? So, copy of the report to *me*, one to the Israeli Embassy. one to the Director of Intelligence Networks, and one to Mr. Mason, care of ODIN."

Ted grinned. "You're the boss."

I paused at the door. Something in my memory was nagging me. I could see the colonel sitting, sagging, still in his light linen jacket. "He's got something," I said. Ted and Gallin stared at me like I was taking leave of my senses. "He's got something," I said again, pointing to my hip. Because I could see it in my mind's eye, bunched up in his pocket. "In his pocket," I said, "in his hip pocket."

I walked back to the living room, holding out my hand to Ted, saying, "Give me some gloves, would you?"

He handed me a pair and I snapped them on, then reached down to the left hip pocket of his jacket and pulled out a cheap cell phone. I glanced at it and handed it to Ted, and he popped it in a bag. Then I reached in the colonel's breast pocket, from which I extracted an iPhone, which I handed to him as well.

"The cheap one has his fingerprints on just some of the numbers. I need to know what those numbers are, and I need you to run them and see how many combinations we can get for phone numbers. Make a list and find out who they belong to."

"Sure thing."

It was turning to late afternoon by the time we stepped out again into the front yard. The blacktop was tinged with bronze under the dappled shadows of the plane trees. Gallin vaulted the car door and slid into the passenger seat, then looked up at me with narrowed eyes.

"That was a lucky guess, right?"

"No, I noticed the lump without realizing it."

"Alex Mason, the Jedi spy."

I leaned on the door. "Learn you will never, if attention you do not pay."

"How do you know only one number was dialed?"

"Because, Gallin, it's a burner. How many times does an intelligence officer use a burner before he throws it away? Besides, I looked, and only about half the numbers had smudges."

"Smart-ass. Turn it around, Yoda. Take the first on your right and go all the way up 38th to Chesapeake Street. Then turn right again."

I climbed behind the wheel, fired up the big brute and turned it around. "Is Mrs. Hirschfield Israeli property too?"

"You bet!"

"So, when you marry me, will you still be Israeli property, or will you become American property?"

Her laughter was a little too shrill, all the way up 38th Street to Chesapeake Street.

Mrs. Hirschfield's house was a thing meant to be admired. Her front lawn, bisected by a gravel path flanked by Lilliputian white picket fences, was like two sheets of green velvet, bordered by exuberant shrubs, magnificent trees and elegant ferns, and where the gravel path met the granite steps that ascended to the colonial veranda, two thuja trees rose like the pillars of Solomon's temple, had Solomon been ecologically aware.

I followed Gallin down the path and up the granite stairs to the glossy white door with a big, shiny brass knob in the center. She rang the bell and instantly the house was filled with voices calling to each other that somebody was ringing at the bell. Eventually the door was opened by a dark-haired girl in jeans and a purple Snoopy sweatshirt. In her hand she held a duster. She gave Gallin the once-over and said to me, "Yeah?"

I let Gallin answer because I knew what was good for me.

"We need to talk to Mrs. Hirschfield."

The girl asked me, "Who should I say?"

I smiled and Gallin said, "Captain Aila Gallin and Captain Alex Mason."

She turned and sashayed away, moving her hips more than you'd think possible without injury to the spine. Gallin turned to me. "You were a captain once, right?"

"I try to forget those days, but I think so."

"What was it, special forces?"

"Something with geometric shapes. Chuck Norris was my commanding officer. He taught me everything I know."

"Hey, don't knock Norris. He's a good guy. You know he was once bitten by a cobra?"

The girl with the double-jointed hips sashayed back and opened the door all the way. "She will see you in the parlor."

She led us across a checkerboard tiled hall, past small Greek statues on small Greek columns, to a small room at the back of the house which had been furnished with the stuff they had left over from the Élysée Palace in Paris.

Mrs. Hirschfield was standing in the middle of the floor and rushed forward when we came in. She had a face that did not take its own beauty seriously, with large brown eyes, a sensitive mouth and high cheekbones. It was a face that was accustomed to laughing, and had learned that laughter was a way to get through bad times.

"Captain Gallin! I *knew* the name was familiar! We met in Tel Aviv! My husband said you were a very promising officer. And, Captain Mason, we haven't met, have we?"

I smiled graciously. "No, I am sure I'd remember."

"Oh, be careful with this one! He's a charmer! Come and sit. What will you have? Carmen, bring coffee! And some biscuits!"

We sat, she and Gallin side by side on the sofa, and I on an overstuffed chair with the kind of shapely legs that would raise a gentleman's eyebrow. Gallin took Mrs. Hirschfield's hand in both of hers and said, "It's Ruth, isn't it? Do you mind if I call you Ruth? I am Aila and this is Alex."

Ruth Hirschfield glanced at me and her beautiful face was disconcerted. Gallin went on.

"Ruth, I am so sorry to have to tell you this. Paul was found dead in his living room today."

She jerked, as though she had been backhanded. Her body rocked and I saw her pupils contract to pinpoints. She said, "No," without emphasis and sank back against the sofa. "No," she said again. "We spoke! We were just speaking. How could he? We were just..."

I stood and while Gallin tried to comfort Ruth I went in

search of Carmen. I eventually found her in the kitchen looking at her cell phone.

"Hey." She looked up but didn't seem particularly surprised to see me. I said, "Forget the coffee. Bring Mrs. Hirschfield some cognac."

"OK."

"Now. Put your telephone down and do it now."

She sighed and put her phone away. "OK."

When I got back Ruth was clinging to Gallin and sobbing convulsively. Carmen was right behind me with a silver tray bearing a couple of decanters of amber liquid and an assortment of cut crystal tumblers and balloons. When she saw the state Ruth was in she did little but raise her eyebrows, deposit the tray and scuttle back to the kitchen and no doubt her phone.

I poured Ruth a generous measure of cognac and handed it to her. She stared at it for a moment like she didn't understand what it was. Then she took it and sat holding it, rocking back and forth for a while until eventually, encouraged by Gallin, she took a sip and that seemed to steady her.

I said, "Is there anyone you want us to call, who can be with you?"

She nodded. "My brother. In the phone book. Harry. He's a doctor."

She pointed at the dresser and Gallin went to get the number and make the call. I sat opposite Ruth. "Mrs. Hirschfield—"

"Ruth," she said in a small voice.

"Ruth, how were things between you and Paul? I know you had recently divorced."

Her lower lip trembled and curled in. Tears spilled from

her eyes again. I gave her my handkerchief and she spoke as she wiped her cheeks and blew her nose.

"We were good. I was playing hard to get, but he had me. He knew it. He was coming to lunch Sunday. He had neglected us for a few years. Work, work, work..." She looked into my eyes and I knew she was begging forgiveness. "A man shouldn't neglect his family, and I thought he should work his way back. But if I had known... Oh God, if I had known!"

Gallin had been talking softly into the telephone. Now she hung up and sat next to Ruth, with her arms around her. To me she said, "He's on his way. He said he'll take ten minutes, fifteen max."

Ruth sat upright, drying her face again. "He was such a good man." She smiled at Gallin. "You knew that. You worked together a few times. He loved his country. He loved his family. The problem with a man with that kind of integrity, people use him. 'Ruth, there aren't enough hours in the day!' That's what he used to say to me. I'd say, 'So spend more of them with me and the kids! Your family!'" She nodded, shook her head and sighed. "That's when he would say, 'Israel still has many enemies, Ruth. To protect my family, first I must protect our country.'" She looked me straight in the eyes. "So you had better tell me," she said, "how did he die?"

FIVE

Steve liked to think of himself as a person without a personality. He liked to think of himself as the ultimate product of the New Age Woke revolution. He was endowed with a normal male body—at least by twenty-first century standards. But because he had not developed his musculature, he easily passed for a girl if he dressed as one. Certainly he was gender-fluid in terms of whether he saw himself as a man or a woman. He was both and neither, depending on what the circumstances required.

Sexually he had no preference. He disliked both equally. He did not enjoy sexual intercourse, and on those occasions when he had been forced to participate he had found it a violent, ugly activity. In fact, when he had meditated on the matter at the suggestion of his first psychotherapist, when he was sixteen, he had concluded that people had sex because they lacked the courage to kill; and that the real drive behind the sex drive was the drive to kill and consume.

Men who saw themselves as real men did it in a brutal, bestial way, pounding you into submission. Women who saw themselves as real women sucked you in and, like a Venus flytrap, dissolved and digested you. He was neither, and so, instead of sexual intercourse, he insinuated himself unseen into your most vulnerable place, and then quietly, simply, snuffed out your life. He often told himself, in his endless internal dialogues, that if his target had been Achilles, he would have become Achilles' sandal, and injected poison into his heel.

He had these thoughts as he sat waiting for his flight at Dulles International Airport. At six fifteen PM precisely he pressed the call button on his dedicated cell phone. It rang once and the colonel's nicotine-stained voice said, "Report."

"The task was successfully accomplished, *Mumiya*."

"In every detail?"

"In every detail. There was some incidental work to be done on request."

"What incidental work?"

"Just some whitewashing and sanitizing. Mila will call you. She said you had foreseen the possibility that the garden outhouse would become dirty, and would need cleaning."

"Oh." She said it like it made sense to her. "Where are you now?"

"At the airport, as you told me. I will arrive in Los Angeles this evening."

"Your contact will meet you at the airport. He will give you further instructions and the tools you will need."

"Yes, *Mumiya*."

He hung up and smiled. He wondered what tools they

would be. He liked to adapt to new and challenging situations. He thought of himself as a shape-shifter or a chameleon. He thought of himself as so many things because he was a person without a personality. That was the way he liked to think of himself.

———

SOME FIVE THOUSAND MILES AWAY, at that very moment, it was one seventeen in the morning on Mokhovaya Street in Moscow. In her small office, opposite Alexander Garden and the Kremlin, Colonel Alexandrina Vitsin put down the phone and sucked on a rollup cigarette at her desk. Her fingertips were stained with nicotine, but she didn't notice anymore. It had been many years since she had stopped noticing the stains on her hands, both metaphoric and real.

She opened the top drawer of her small desk and extracted a photograph of twenty youths in their late teens. They all wore cadet uniforms. Ten boys, ten girls. She had circled two with black pen. One, the boy, was startlingly handsome. He had platinum blond hair, chiseled, regular features, and he stood tall and athletic. And though you could not see it in the photograph, she remembered well his languid, arrogant blue eyes. Peter, Peter Belov. She had hated him from the first day she had set eyes on him in the academy. But he was a supremely good operative, and he had enjoyed the protection of powerful people. Yet she had always known that sooner or later he would betray her, and Mother Russia.

The other was Maria Pyryeva, the great love of her life.

Just as she had detested Peter, she had adored Maria with a passion that transcended everything. Nothing in Colonel Alexandrina's life had ever compared to the unendurable passion she had felt for Maria. There had been times she had wanted to tear at her beautiful face, take a razor to her, throw her in a cell until she rotted to death. Those times were all when she had seen how she looked at Peter.

But other times, most times, she evoked in the colonel's chest a warmth and a tenderness she had never known before. Then she would call for her and they would spend happy hours together, eating strawberries, drinking champagne. Talking. She had taught Maria so much, led her, guided her, given her life meaning.

And the ungrateful bitch had betrayed her, with that arrogant Rus! That aristocratic, sneering bastard! Suddenly she screamed and with vicious savagery she crushed her cigarette into Maria's face.

The door opened after a moment and a lieutenant peered in. "Colonel?"

She dismissed him with her fingers, stared at the photograph, charred and filthy, and thought of Maria's beautiful face and body, burned, disfigured and utterly destroyed in Brazil. She was irrevocably lost, irretrievable, dead.

The colonel wept. It was a noisy, ugly affair that lasted ten minutes. Then she went to her small bathroom and washed the tears and the saliva from her face. When she was done she considered her face in the mirror. Her thin lips, her hard chin and her small eyelashes. It was a face she had used to hate, but over time she had grown to like. It was like her, ugly but indomitable and indestructible.

Vodka. A shot of vodka would settle her, and then she

would continue in her labor, wreaking bloody vengeance on everyone who had failed her or betrayed her, or stood in her way.

SOME SEVEN HOURS LATER, when it was one AM in DC and eight AM in Moscow, it was nine PM in Los Angeles and Steve was sitting at a table on the terrace at the Perch, on Pershing Square. Sitting opposite him, in a cream linen suit with a pink shirt and slip-on Italian shoes with no socks, was George Malkin. George, despite his clothes, had an overtly masculine manner. Few would have known he was gay. He was sipping a dry martini and speaking in a low rumble.

"I met with the senator in his private office early this afternoon. We have become friends over the last few weeks. He has agreed to spend the weekend with me discussing his campaign strategy and ways in which I can help him. I told him it would be just me and him, a companion to keep the pool warm and my personal secretary, Karen Wilkens, who harbors a deep fascination for him. That will be you. He liked that." His eyes flicked over Steve with a certain insolent pleasure. "I hope what the colonel says about you is true. We will practice tonight. You had better be convincing." He sneered suddenly. "I must say, even dressed as a man you don't look much like one. You have no beard?"

Steve blinked once. It was the only movement he made. "It is a rare genetic condition. I have no hair except on my head."

"Your voice is neutral," George observed to himself. "On the phone I could not tell if you were male or female."

"I am sure you can trust the colonel's choice."

"No doubt, but if this goes wrong *I* will pay the price, not the colonel. So forgive me if I make double sure."

"I have never failed yet. Nor has my work ever been criticized."

"How many jobs have you done?"

"Twenty-six. And five before that out of curiosity." He smiled and George's scalp prickled in spite of himself. "Four men are serving life sentences for those experiments as we speak."

"Was that...?"

"Part of the experiment? Yes. I wanted to know if I could get away with it scot-free. The frames were flawless."

George cleared his throat and nodded. "Right," he said, trying hard to conceal his discomfort. "So, we need to make sure the senator takes the bait. Our research suggests he has a weakness for pretty, feminine young women. With the nominations coming up he might be on his guard and reluctant to take risks, so you're going to have to encourage him."

"I'll do my part. He won't be able to resist me. But you need to offer him the guarantees that there is no risk of being found out. How are you going to do that?"

"I've taken care of that already. I told him I want the White House to start relaxing sanctions against Russia because I have substantial investments there, investments that will flourish when the sanctions are lifted. I want him, when he is elected, to propose a negotiated settlement in the Ukraine." He spread his hands, waving them in a "yadda yadda" gesture. "Russia keeps the Donbas, Ukraine gets her independence and no NATO. That way they can relax the sanctions and my investments make a killing. In exchange I offer him a percentage. He is interested.

"Meanwhile, when you meet tomorrow, you make the attraction obvious, I spot it and I suggest we spend the day on my yacht, miles away from any prying photographers."

"Will he fear blackmail?"

George shook his head. "No, it does not arise. Because I am not asking him to do anything he hasn't already said he's going to do in private conversations anyway. I have deliberately tailored my requests to coincide with his political posture. As far as he's concerned, he is being bribed to do what he already wants to do. He'll be laughing up his sleeve."

"Until the knife comes out."

"Yeah, until then."

"What about his wife?"

"Simple. He will tell her what he believes to be the case. He is coming to my house in Eastern Malibu for a weekend of campaign talk and planning. She will not be a problem. From what my sources tell me, she will find plenty of ways to entertain herself while he is gone.

"But instead of staying at the mansion in Malibu, we will discretely move to the yacht. He will be happy to go incognito, because he does not want to be seen by anyone. While we are on the yacht Sergey will—"

"Who is Sergey?"

"One of our operatives. None of your concern. He will take the senator's car and leave it in the parking lot of the Skin Gentlemen's Club on South Robertson Boulevard."

Steve looked out at the sparkling city and smiled the way a killer worm might smile. "He stayed at the house for the day, the meeting went well and he left in the evening. You didn't see him after that. It is a great loss, not just for America but for the world."

George shrugged and signaled the waiter. "If anyone ever thinks to ask. After all," he turned and smiled at Steve, "there will be no body. Just a vanishing senator."

SIX

SOME HOURS EARLIER, WHILE THE SUN WAS STILL laying a dappled copper sheen across the blacktop on Chesapeake Street NW, Aila Gallin, with that same late, dappled light lying across her face, sat on the hood of my Mk4, crossed her ankles and crossed her arms.

"He didn't commit suicide."

I thrust my hands deep in my pockets and looked up at the cool, pale-green leaves.

"So he was murdered. What can we extrapolate from that? A, that the list is in fact a hit list; B, that something very powerful prevented him from fighting off his killer—"

"Or, he did not expect his killer to kill him. It was a surprise."

I nodded but made an annoying strained noise and screwed up my eyes. "I thought of that," I said, "but then you have to ask yourself, why did he have his weapon in his hand?" I shook my head at the leaves. "No, he knew they were coming for him. He sat in that chair, in the dark corner with the drapes half closed, to wait for his killer. He left the French doors open in the hope he would come in from the glare into a darkened room and he would have a chance to take him out. But that didn't happen. Instead he just sat there, and didn't fight back. What made him do that?"

"You know, don't you?"

I shook my head. "No, if I did I'd tell you. After all, you are in charge of this investigation."

"Dick head."

"We must arise and go now," I said, walking round to the driver's door, "and go to Innisfree—"

"Where?"

As she climbed in I fired up the engine and moved off.

"And a small cabin build there, of clay and wattles made; Nine bean-rows will I have there, a hive for the honey-bee; And live alone in the bee-loud glade..."

"Where are we going, Mason?"

"To see my friend Dolly." She made a "mh" sound which I ignored. "Because point C which we can extrapolate from Colonel Hirschfield's murder is that, if Dolly put a piece of paper in my pocket with his name on it this morning, and he was killed this afternoon, she knew that was going to happen."

"Where does she live?"

"In a less exalted neighborhood."

"That narrows it down."

"19th Street in Mount Pleasant."

"That's a good neighborhood."

"But it's not exalted. She lives in a three-story house converted to apartments. She has the ground floor. If she's not home yet, we'll wait for her."

19th Street NW was a leafy, middle-class street of elegant Edwardian houses owned by middle-class people who were not as well off as they had been when the houses were built. Back then the basements housed the kitchen and the servants' quarters. Now they were converted into apartments and housed the tenants who were helping you to pay off your second mortgage.

For others, as was the case with Dolly's landlord, the entire house had been converted into one and two-bedroom apartments that were not small but *bijoux*, and were all the new, young middle class could afford.

Gallin was staring at the houses with an outraged face that was going to explode if she didn't say something.

"Have you ever noticed," she said suddenly, climbing on her soapbox, "how a hundred and fifty years ago, one middle-class man could keep a family, with servants, in a decent family home, and give his kids a good, private education? And now that things are so much better, both parents have to work and they can't afford to put their kids through college?"

"I had noticed that, Gallin, yes."

"You want to tell me how that is progress?"

"Not right now, no. That is her house there, and that Toyota was parked outside Helen Troy's mansion this morning. Let's go."

She scowled at me and climbed out. As we walked toward the house she said, "It's an assault on the family, and on family values. Families are not, and should not be, cost-effective."

"Ours won't be, Gallin," I said, as we climbed the steps to the porch and rang the bell. "We'll buy a vast house in

Wyoming. We'll have fourteen servants and five kids and we'll teach the kids to ride and shoot at the age of two. Then we can live off bison and homemade beer."

There was no expression on her face. Nobody answered the door. So I rang again. Nobody answered again. I had a sinking feeling in my gut and pulled my Swiss Army knife from my pocket. I glanced down the road, but Gallin was ahead of me.

"We're third from the end. I'll go down the alley and vault the fence. Give me three minutes, then go in."

She was gone before I could answer, sprinting down to the alley. I counted to one hundred and eighty, rammed the screwdriver into the lock and turned.

I stepped into a tight hallway that smelt of furniture polish and fresh paint. On my right was the door to the ground-floor apartment. I knocked a couple of times and heard nothing, so I gave that lock the same Swiss Army treatment and let myself into a large, sunlit room that served as living room, dining room and kitchen. There was even a corner with a desktop computer, filing cabinet and printer. I figured maybe Gallin had a point.

I looked out the kitchen window and saw her scrambling over a fence that was probably higher than she'd expected, so I opened the door to the bedroom. The last thing I saw before I blacked out was a woman lying on the bed fully clothed. She had a pillow over her face and there was a singed, black hole in the middle of the pillow.

Then I felt a lot of jarring pain in my head and I vanished into oblivion.

According to John Grinder and Richard Bandler, consciousness arises when things are different. When everything is the same, like perpetual darkness, consciousness fades away. But if you have a constant body temperature of, say, sixty-eight Fahrenheit, and somebody throws a jug of water at thirty-nine Fahrenheit in your face, that is different and consciousness arises again.

It also makes you splutter and gasp, and you become aware of the blunt axe wedged in your skull.

"Did you see who hit you?"

"What? No. In the bedroom. I think it's Dolly."

"Shit!"

While I got painfully to my feet she went to the bedroom door and looked in. I stood by her side, then pushed past her and carefully lifted the pillow off the woman's face. There was a neat, 9mm entry wound in the middle of her forehead. Her pretty green eyes were closed, screwed tight, and the pillow behind her head was saturated with fresh blood. Gallin said:

"The bedclothes are rumpled, the lamp on the night-stand," she pointed, "the shade is askew. Like it was knocked over and stood up again."

I called Ted.

"Yo!"

"You got another team?"

"I've got a couple of guys."

"I need you at 19th Street NW in Mount Pleasant, as soon as you can."

"What is it?"

"It's a dead body, shot in the head."

"I'll send over a couple of guys now. I'll be there in about an hour."

I hung up and called Nero.

"Yes, Alex."

"Helen Troy's personal assistant, the woman who slipped me the list, has been murdered in her apartment, shot in the head with a 9mm round through a pillow. I do not want anyone, *anyone*, setting foot in this apartment aside from me, Gallin and our forensic team. Nobody, not Israeli intelligence, not the MPD, not the Secret Service. Nobody but me, Gallin, Ted and his team."

"Was it the same killer?"

"I don't think so, and she was not on the list. The killer was here when I arrived. He pistol-whipped me from behind and got away."

"That's unfortunate. Keep me informed."

I hung up and Gallin spoke from behind me, leaning on the doorjamb looking into the bedroom.

"It was messy, a last-minute, risky decision."

"I agree. She was killed because I went to see Helen Troy."

"So she knew the killer and wanted to alert you before her boss was killed."

I nodded silently, thinking it through. "How did she know about me? What made her pick me? Why not the cops?"

"Maybe she thought she was being followed, her phone was tapped, whatever, and that's why she did the whole elaborate bumping into you affair." She thought about it a moment and shrugged. "And maybe she was right and it wasn't your visit to Troy's house at all, but she was seen bumping into you on the train."

I frowned. "How the hell did she know I was coming back from New York on that train?"

She made a face and raised her eyebrows high. "You are attracting a lot of attention, my friend. It'll be a desk job for you pretty soon."

"We need to think about who knows me. And we need to go over this house with a fine-toothed comb. The list she gave me was a photocopy. Where did the original come from?"

Gallin ran her fingers through her hair, like she was trying to stimulate her brain. "Did she copy it at work?"

"Why would Senator Troy have a hit list with her own name on it?"

"Fair point. So she either copied it somewhere else or she stole it and copied it here on that three-in-one."

I went over to the work station and dropped into the chair. The computer was set on a small wooden desk with three drawers down one side, and beside it was a gray and cream steel filing cabinet. Gallin said, "You got a copy of the list on you?"

I pulled it out of my wallet and gave it to her. While she examined it I tried the drawers in the desk. They were all locked. The filing cabinet gave the same result.

"See these two dots?" She showed me and I nodded. "That means it was stapled to another sheet of paper."

I looked up at her face, thinking—trying to think— "An explanatory note? Details about each person?"

"Was it removed just to copy it and then put back?"

"There's got to be a key somewhere. Where's her purse?"

Gallin found her purse in the kitchen, and using two pieces of kitchen paper, she brought it over and emptied it on the desk. There was a bunch of keys and a little experimentation gave us a small, brass chub-style key for the desk and a small, steel Yale-type key for the filing cabinet.

What she had locked so carefully in her desk turned out to be little more than staples, paper and ink for the printer, rubber bands, pens and spare notebooks with nothing written in them.

I used one of the pens to switch on the computer, just in case her killer had been snooping around her desk too, and came immediately on the welcome page requiring a password.

"The IT department will have to deal with this. You got anything?"

She had been very quiet for a while and I looked up at her, leaning on the open top drawer of the cabinet.

"Most of it is just memos," she said absently, "press releases, correspondence with supporters...," she was quiet for a while, reading, "ten bucks from here, fifty bucks from Buck Jones promising more where that came from if she'll swear to protect the Second Amendment..." She lapsed into silence again. Then, "'We are sliding back to the dark ages before the liberation of the '70s. Will she come out and declare that she supports women's sovereignty over their own bodies?'"

She dropped the sheaf of papers she was holding back into the top drawer, slammed it shut and opened the middle one. Outside I heard a car pull up and went to the windows to see who it was. I recognized Lu and Gus, two guys from our forensic department, and went to open the door.

We greeted each other with "Heys" and "His" and I showed them into the apartment. I closed the door and told them, "The victim is in the bedroom, on the bed. Looks like the killer used a cushion to stop her screaming, and may have had a suppressor on the gun. I want every minutest detail you can give me about this guy. In particular, he may have left fingerprints on her arms, face, body. Start with the bedroom, but I want the whole apartment gone over with a microscope."

Lu jerked his big head at the computer and the filing cabinet. "You touched that?"

"With a pen."

"For sure? What about the files?"

Gallin said absently, "I'll give you samples of my prints."

Lu nodded. "Good enough. Please don't come into the bedroom. Please don't go anywhere else, and please leave as soon as possible." He glanced at Gallin and then back at me. "Every moment you are here you make our work more difficult."

"I know. We're nearly done."

They shuffled away to the bedroom and set about their job. I went to the window and looked out at the street, still and silent. The only movement was the occasional twitch of a leaf on the plane trees.

How had she got hold of my name? The logical assumption was that she had got it from her boss, via security connections. But her boss had not known who I was. So that avenue was closed. What set of circumstances had put that list and my name in the possession of a fairly small-time personal assistant to an also-ran contender for nomination?

Gallin said suddenly, "The juicy stuff is obviously at the house. This is just the small stuff that she was allowed to do from home. But even this," she held up a handful of papers, "is there such a thing as a politician with standards, ethics, morals?"

I smiled. "It's like a snake with legs. We call it a lizard. A politician with morals is called a martyr. How bad is it?"

She shrugged. "Nah, it's not that bad. You see worse at the White House, but even at this level, you know, you can see that everything is on the table and nothing is on the altar. Nothing is sacred..."

She trailed off. I smiled. "Everything is on the table and nothing on the altar. I like that." She flipped a page and there was a poised tension about her that made me ask, "What is it?"

She crossed the room and handed me two pieces of paper that were stapled together. I took them and stared at the first page. It was the list, the original, written in pen. Helen Troy's name was underscored and, as Gallin had predicted, there were two holes top left where the original staple had been. These had been partially covered with a new staple which was holding a second page. I flipped over and looked at the list of three names that had been added, two of which had been crossed out. The first was Peter Belov, the second was Maria Pyryeva, who had also been crossed out. The third name was Alex Masson. That had been underscored, like Helen's, and had two exclamation marks beside it.

SEVEN

Senator Jim Reed had a French château on North Rexford Drive, in Beverly Hills. It was an understated affair with only seven bedrooms and a severe absence of gaudy decorations on the exterior. Beyond the wrought-iron gates, which he had bought in Lyon and shipped back to Los Angeles, there was merely an asphalt drive and a few trees. The façade of the house, aside from a scrolled pediment above a small wrought-iron balcony on the second floor, had only green wooden shutters to break its stoic, stone monotony.

Senator Jim Reed had always had a sense of admiration for the French, which he knew was not shared by his party as a whole. But in his view, in spite of their tendency to run away in wars, have extramarital affairs and talk like they were gay, they had a lot to offer in the way of good wine and exquisite food, cool architecture and philosophers that were easy to quote. He had used a few in his speeches and they always went down well.

He smiled at himself in his dressing-room mirror as he tied his silk cravat and tucked it under his crisp, Jermyn Street white shirt. He nodded, as though to a large crowd, and pointed a finger like a Colt Revolver.

"Was it not Jean-Paul Sartre who said, 'Man is *condemned* to be free! Because once thrown into the world, *he is responsible* for everything he does!"

He shrugged on his Gieves & Hawkes blazer, tugged at his yellow handkerchief so that it spilled a little out of his pocket, grabbed his overnight bag and trotted down the broad, semi-spiral staircase fashioned from white marble, wrought iron and brass, that had once graced the hallway of an actual French château, in France.

He stopped dead halfway down on seeing his wife, who had once seemed beautiful to him. She emerged from the morning room (or, as he called it, the *sale du matin*) in a salmon pink robe that did nothing to conceal her considerable attributes. In her hand she held the first of a number of gin and orange cocktails she would consume that morning.

"We *are*," he said, and his voice echoed under the vaulted ceiling, "our choices. Jean-Paul Sartre said that."

"Go tell it to the Stars and Stripes. My choice is to drink until I forget what an asshole I married."

He continued trotting down the stairs, adjusting his cuffs as he went. "That asshole you married just got listed in the Fortune Five Hundred and is paying for your lifestyle. You'd be wise to remember that, sweet cheeks."

She watched him reach the bottom of the stairs and asked, "Where are you going?"

He regarded her for a moment and sighed. "I told you last night. I have a meeting with George Malkin. We are discussing finance and strategy. I am going to be president, and you are going to be the First Lady. Remember?"

"I was too drunk to listen. When will you be back?"

He crossed the terracotta tiled floor to adjust his cravat at the umbrella stand.

"Maybe tonight. Maybe tomorrow. It depends on how the meeting goes."

"Make it tomorrow and I'll get the pool boy to stay over and keep me company."

The slap he gave her echoed across the cold, stone hall. It was not hard enough to move her, or make her drop her drink. She stood for a moment with her eyes closed. When she opened them there was hatred behind the small, black pupils.

"Is that how much you care? You hit like a French girl."

"You had better shape up, Nancy. This ride goes to the White House. I'd like you to come with me. You've got a good family, a good background and you've got class, when you're not drunk. But if you think my team will allow you, in this state," he gestured at her with disgust, "to stand before the nation as First Lady, as the president's wife, you have got another think coming, sweetheart."

Her face seemed to sag into despair. "You used to love me. At least I thought you did."

"Look at what I am offering you, for God's sake! How damned ungrateful can you be?"

In her mind she told him, she screamed at him, that she would swap all of it, from the White House to the convertible Aston Martin on the drive, for one sincere caress. But the sourness in her mouth killed the words like poison and she never spoke them. Instead she said, "Words are loaded pistols. You know who said that?"

He sneered and raised an eyebrow. "Mickey Spillane? You want to try doing some serious reading, sweetheart. You might learn something."

Outside a horn blared twice and he moved toward the door. Her voice stopped him as he reached for the handle.

"Jean-Paul Sartre." He stopped and looked at her. There was something oddly territorial in his stare. She smiled. "Jean Paul Sartre said it, in an essay on literature. You see," she said with sudden savagery, "I *have* an education. I actually *went* to a good school! I didn't crawl out of the gutter, and I don't need to *pretend!*"

He stepped out and closed the door. He heard the glass smash on the other side and resolved to talk to Brice, his lawyer, about a divorce as soon as he got back from Malibu. Then he shut her out of his thoughts and focused on the Bentley Continental that was parked just in front of him in the drive. Behind the wheel was George Malkin, leaning across the seat to greet him.

He slung his bag on the backseat, climbed into the solid, safe luxury of the car and closed the door with a satisfying thud.

"I need to get me one of these babies."

George, amiably complacent, pulled out onto Rexford Drive and cruised south toward Santa Monica Boulevard.

"They're nice," he said. "I thought you had one. You know, I have been thinking a lot about your career." He turned and gave Reed a very white, twenty-thousand-dollar smile. "I *really* want you to be president. I mean, you are the guy. You are *the guy!* You are."

Reed laughed. "Come on!" He tried to sound self-deprecating, but he didn't try very hard.

"No, I am serious, Jim. You have everything it takes, money, status, connections. You are well respected in Congress, the press likes you and the people love you. You say all the right things and, what is so refreshing, you *mean* them!"

Jim gave his head a small twitch. "Well, I do care about our country, George."

"I know you do, Jim. And I'll tell you another thing. You were one of the very few to come out of that Russian suitcase bomb affair smelling of roses."

Jim cleared his throat. "Yeah, well, thank the Lord all of that is behind us."

George shook his head, eyes on the road. "I tell you, when the feces hit the fan there was barely a man who could hold his head up. Seemed like everybody had their hand in the Russian cash register at some point. But not you. You stood tall and condemned the Russians, and all the traitors who, *despite* the shame of the whole Ukrainian war, were still dealing behind closed doors with the Putin regime."

An uncomfortable silence settled on them for a moment, till Reed said, "Well, you know what Jean-Paul Sartre said—"

"Whose she?"

"French philosopher, the father of existentialism."

"Oh, you mean John Paul Sartre."

"No, it's J-E-A-N—"

"Yeah, but the French pronounce that John. So what did he say?"

Reed sighed. "Never mind. So what's the plan for today?"

"Well, you know what? I was thinking, you have a real high profile right now. And we have no need of the press, and all those boys over in DC, knowing that we are putting our heads together. Am I right?"

"Usually."

George laughed. "Damn right, I am! So I thought, tinted windows," he pointed around at the car windows, "nobody knows you're with me, nobody sees you arrive at my pad in Malibu, and, for extra privacy I thought, why don't we take the yacht out. I have a little friend over who will keep me company, and meantime my secretary is plumb crazy about you. She is smart as a whip, pretty as a peach and she just never stops talking about Senator Reed!" He threw back his head and laughed. "And," he added after a moment, "the soul of discretion. I have had a couple of situations, know what I mean, and she has been superb. Not my type, Jim. But I know she's your type. Pettit, blonde, blue eyes."

He winked and Jim smiled as he looked at the road ahead. The weekend was shaping up. A pretty young girl whom George could control might be just the thing to erase the nasty taste of Nancy from his mouth.

They took the Pacific Coast Highway and followed the curve of the bay under the vast dome of a perfect blue sky, where a scattering of white clouds sailed like dinghies in the breeze.

"This," said George, spreading his hands, "should be done in a convertible with a pretty lady by your side. Preferably *not* your wife. But I really do want this weekend to be private. Not just because we might get up to a few games your wife and your voters might disapprove of, but because we need to be focused on strategies and moves that could make you the most powerful man in the world, Jim. President James Reed—sounds good, donnit?"

"It does that, George."

"Sounds like a name that will go down in history."

At Malibu Sands he turned onto Carbon Resort Terrace and began to climb through rich, green hills dotted with palm trees and tall pines until, at the top of a hill which overlooked Malibu Sands and the vast Pacific, they came to a huge, walled mansion with a solid steel, electronic gate. The wall was solid stone topped with broken glass, and over the top all you could see was a couple of domed roofs, more palms and more pines.

The gate rolled back after a moment, and they rolled in, up a winding asphalt drive to a palatial home shaded by exotic gardens and fronted by a circle with an elaborate Renaissance fountain showing Poseidon squirting water at a dolphin.

Three broad marble steps led up to an arched doorway flanked by rose gardens, and standing on the path, looking very pretty and demure, was a petite young woman with blonde hair tied back in a ponytail, a pink cotton dress and a light cardigan.

"Oh, that's nice. Karen has come to greet us." George grinned at Reed. "Told you she's crazy to meet you. Just your type, huh?"

"How well you know me."

"C'mon, I'll introduce you."

They climbed out of the car and Karen stepped forward, nodding to George, but holding out her hand to Reed.

"Mr. Malkin. Senator Reed, may I shake your hand? I hope you don't mind, I just wanted to tell you how much I admire what you are doing, and your devotion to our ancient liberties and freedoms."

Senator Jim Reed smiled and seemed to swell. "Well, little lady, I am really flattered." He turned to George. "You better keep her tied down, George, or I might just steal her from you!" Karen giggled and blushed. James addressed her in a deeper, gruffer voice. "Well, I hope we'll have the opportunity to discuss all my policies while I am here, Karen."

"Oh, I would love that, sir. To hear it from your very lips."

George was already pushing inside. Calling over his shoulder, "Come on, Jim! We have a lot to talk about. Karen, we'll have coffee by the pool, and arrange everything for the yacht. You'll be coming with us." He laughed. "So pack a bikini!"

Reed held her eye for a moment, then practically growled, "I'll catch you later."

They changed into beach clothes and sat beside the turquoise pool in the shade of palm trees and parasols, and drank strong black coffee.

George shook his head. "I don't know what you see in them. She's like a thin strip of raw fish. I prefer something with some substance. Something you can grab a hold of."

Jim shrugged. "It's the fact that they are so frail. You crush them and they break. It is total domination."

"Power and control."

"The two most powerful aphrodisiacs known to man."

"To each his own. Listen, Jim, something that I should have thought of sooner, but I've had so much on my mind.

The Range Rover and the Porsche are both at the vineyard upstate. And Sunday night I am going to have to leave at five in the morning to prepare for a meeting at nine AM Monday in San Diego."

"No problem. I'll have my driver bring my car up."

"Exactly. Just have him drop it off and we'll get him home safe and sound. He doesn't need to know you're out on the yacht, right?"

"Right. Got to hand it to you, George. You think of everything."

They talked for another half hour about whom they could bribe, who was vulnerable to blackmail and whether Helen Troy was a serious threat—George was firmly of the opinion that Jim need not worry about either Helen or Frank Costello—and then Karen appeared, with her hands clasped in front of her belly, and told them everything was ready and they could make tracks for the yacht just as soon as they liked. So they transferred back to the Bentley where Jim sat in the front passenger seat and Karen sat behind. Jim frowned.

"Didn't you say somebody else was coming...?"

"Oh, she's on the yacht already, preparing lunch. She's Cubana, and likes to make Cuban dishes. So listen, Jim, talk to me about the Russians. How do you feel about all these punitive sanctions against Russia?"

"Well, we can't be seen to condone—"

"I mean, take an entrepreneur like me, creating wealth, jobs and opportunities. Those sanctions against Russia hurt me as much as they hurt the Russian oligarchs. You know what I'm saying?"

Unsure of his ground, Reed nodded and said, "I have often thought the same thing."

"So you would suggest a dialogue with Russia—"

"Exactly. Dialogue leads to understanding."

"And meantime we can leave channels open so that our boys can sell essential goods, goods that people need for survival, to the Russians and the Ukrainians alike. Am I wrong? I mean, the man on the street is not at fault here, and should not be made to pay for his leader's mistakes."

"Exactly," said Reed, trying to make it sound like it was his idea, "our entrepreneurs should be free to sell to Ukraine *and* Russia."

George chuckled. "You are my kind of politician, Jim, endlessly flexible and adaptable. I admire that in a politician."

They left the Bentley in the parking lot beside the pier where they were met by a tall, tanned man with very short hair and tattoos on his arms. George gave him the key to the Bentley and told him, "I'll call you." The man took the car and drove off back toward Santa Monica, while George led Karen and Reed down onto the beach, where a small launch had been drawn up on the sand.

"You guys get aboard," said George, laughing for no particular reason, "I'll push her out," and as they climbed in he heaved the boat out into the small waves.

EIGHT

WE WERE SITTING IN NERO'S OFFICE. GALLIN WAS one of the rare few who had ever been allowed to enter what we called Valhalla, and that had as much to do with Nero's friendship with Gabriel Gallin as it did with her past record of support and loyalty.

Nero had been reading a couple of reports when we entered, and after a moment, as we sat, he laid them down and pinched the bridge of his nose.

"First," he said, "facts. Dolores Scott, Helen Troy's personal assistant, presented extensive bruising on her arms and on her face. Though her assailant wore gloves and left no prints, it was possible to gauge his approximate size. He is a large, heavy, strong man with an *iron* grip." Nero clenched his large, right fist to illustrate. "However, no such bruising was evident on Colonel Hirschfield's person. On the contrary, the murder was contrived so skillfully that it was almost impossible to conclude it was not suicide. Of course one was left with the discomfiture of the unlikelihood of the shot, and also the fact that he was a man with every reason to live.

"Yet, I asked Ted to look for pressure marks or bruises upon his right hand, particularly on the soft tissue around the back of the thumb and on the index finger."

Gallin said, "Oh, that's good. Where the killer held his hand to the gun. The recoil would have left pressure marks."

"Thank you. That revealed not only pressure from another hand, which naturally after death did not spring back, it also revealed a peculiar, uneven pattern of gunshot residue."

"Brilliant."

"Again, thank you. And we can extrapolate from the pressure exerted on Colonel Hirschfield's hand, and from the size of the imprint, that the colonel's killer was small and not particularly strong."

"So he was drugged," I said.

"It is hard to see how else it could have been carried out. The autopsy did reveal a minute pinprick in the neck that might have been used to administer some form of nondepolarization neuromuscular blockers—"

Gallin's eyebrows had shot up on her brow. I smiled at her and said, "Something like curare, a paralyzing agent."

Nero added, "Which leaves no trace in the blood. Because a small amount is sufficient to paralyze a large man, it can be administered barely leaving a trace. Once the victim is paralyzed you can do with him what you like. However, the point of interest here is that we have two killers. One of them is brutish and not very efficient. The other is small, not very strong, very subtle, and experienced enough to keep his calm and perform his task almost to perfection.

"Question: are they working for the same employer? Evidently they are both connected with the list. Alex."

I had raised a finger. "Dolores Scott was not actually on the list, so it would seem likely that she was killed as a punishment for contacting me, by the available muscle, while the pro makes his way methodically through the list."

"We must assume you are being watched. Not only are you on the list, but she was killed after she made contact with you. This fact may play to our advantage. For the rest of it I believe you are probably right. So we can conclude with some degree of certainty that our smaller, more subtle killer is currently either preparing to kill Helen Troy, on his way to New York to assassinate Senator Costello or on his way to Los Angeles in pursuit of James Reed. We are currently trying to establish the whereabouts of Priti Anand and Johannes de Jong, but so far without success."

"The other fact," said Gallin, "sir, forgive me for interrupting—"

"I doubt I shall, but continue anyway."

"Thank you, sir, as the fact that both Mason and Troy's names were underscored. I would say that that, right there—"

"Means they have been prioritized as targets. Yes, thank you, Captain Gallin. That was, in fact, my next point. Without information to the contrary we must assume that the assassin's next target will be either Helen Troy or Alex. Thus it would make sense to have you sitting on the senator's house. If she is willing then you should be in the house and traveling with her as permanent bodyguards. If she is not willing then you must improvise the next best thing. I will attempt to bring pressure to bear from her party, but I suggest when you leave here you go directly to see her and explain the situation. If she wishes you can arrange a meeting with me and I will stress the gravity of the risk."

I nodded. It made sense. "What about Costello and Reed? They need to be alerted."

"We have asked the Bureau to cooperate with us and they are sending special agents to talk to them and their security teams."

"The next order of business then, sir, is for us to go to Helen Troy's house and..." I spread my hands. "And wait?"

"That is about all we can do at present." He raised a finger. "There is one small fact that offers little hope at present. Dolores Scott scratched her killer. Minute traces of skin and blood were found under her nails. Clearly, with your arrival, he didn't have time either to recover the list or to clean her nails—assuming the thought occurred to him. The lab is attempting to draw a profile from it. They are not hopeful, and even if they do there is little chance we will find him on CODIS. But there we are, we are trying."

WE ARRIVED at Senator Troy's place a little over an hour later. The sun had dipped behind the horizon but it was still close enough to touch the sky with blue, and the few scattered clouds with red. I stood and looked at the dome of heaven slipping into darkness, while Gallin rang at the door. It was opened after a moment by the same well-dressed maid who'd opened it before, only this time she gave us a look that said we really were very naughty and mommy was going to be very cross.

"She is no gonna want to see you."

I came up behind Gallin and said, "She is going to *have* to see us, or I'll have the National Guard put tanks in her front and backyard." I gave her a pleasant smile and added, "I am not joking. Please go and tell her we are here."

She didn't invite me in this time. She left us standing on the doorstep and disappeared toward the dining room. I returned my attention to the sky, but all the clouds that had been red a moment before, now looked like they had been stained with blackcurrant juice.

The brisk, angry tapping of heels brought me back to Great Falls. Her voice echoed slightly in the ample hall.

"This really is intolerable! We are having dinner!"

I turned to face her. "Colonel Paul Hirschfield isn't."

She screwed up her brow and scowled at me. "*What?*"

"Do you know him? Colonel Paul Hirschfield, of the Israeli—"

"I know who Paul Hirschfield is, Mr. Mason. He is a friend of the family."

I stepped right up to the door, beside Gallin. "Then I am very sorry to have to give you this news while you're having dinner. Colonel Hirschfield has been murdered."

Bother her hands went to her mouth, but she only covered it with her fingers. "Paul? How?" She struggled with a few *W*s and settled on, "Why? This is awful! When did this happen?"

"Can we come in, Senator?"

She stared at me a moment like I had asked an outrageous question, then shifted her gaze to Gallin. Finally she blinked and said, "Yes, of course."

She led us to her office and we sat on the cream sofas she had perpendicular to her walnut desk. Gallin sat next to her, half-turned to face her, and I sat opposite. She had gone very still and quiet, and now said, "Is this to do with your list?"

"He was on it."

"He was a very well-connected man," she said. "He was likeable and honest, and had friends everywhere, from the local storekeeper to the president. He didn't differentiate. He supported our party, not because he shared our political views, but because we are more vocal in our support for Israel."

She licked her lips and looked down at her hands, clasped between her knees. You could sense how her sadness had been set aside for later, and her mind was working on the problem in hand. It made you wonder if "later" ever came.

"This is an attack on the party, then."

Gallin answered. "Could you explain that please, Senator?"

"Who are you?"

I answered, "Forgive me. This is Captain Aila Gallin, my partner. She is attached to the Pentagon. How do you see this as an attack on the party?"

"Three candidates for nomination, two financial backers and an influential supporter. After a blow like that the party would be crippled for years, and perceived in the public eye as weak, unable to defend itself."

Gallin asked, "How well did you know the colonel?"

She shrugged. "Socially. He was like everybody's favorite uncle. He was always admonishing me that you can't please everybody. The more allowed Arab oil to influence American policy, the more power we gave to Islam. It was his constant refrain. 'The West does not understand Islam.'"

She smiled. "'Westerners think with their stomachs, Jews think with their hearts, Muslims think what they are told to think.'" She shook her head. "I used to tell him, 'Paul, you cannot talk like that. This is a new age of tolerance and dialogue.'"

Gallin snorted, "And he would reply, 'Dialogue with an AK47 always ends the same way. The AK47 is always right.'"

The senator assessed Gallin carefully. "You knew him?"

"Yeah, I knew him. He will be missed by a lot of people. You think his views on American policy in the Middle East might have had something to do with his murder?"

The senator spread her hands above her knees. "I am not in possession of the facts, Captain Gallin. I can't possibly comment." She shrugged her eyebrows and gave a humorless laugh. "The embassy of Israel in Washington DC is not the same as the embassy of Iceland in New Zealand. You don't become the senior intelligence officer of the Israeli Embassy in DC without making a few serious enemies along the way. Especially when you are as uncompromising in your views as Paul was. But please don't ask me to move from the general to the particular, because I just don't know. All I can say is that on the face of it, this seems to be an attack on the party as a whole."

I reached in my pocket and took out the photocopy of the first page, which Dolores Scott had given me early that morning.

"Can you think of any reason why your name should be underscored there?"

She ran her eyes over the paper several times. "No idea at all. How did you get a hold of this?"

"Where was your PA yesterday, Senator?"

"Yesterday? She took the day off. She said she wanted to visit family in Baltimore. Why?"

"And where is she now, Senator?"

"I have no idea. At home, I assume. *Why?* What is it with Dolly?"

"Dolores was murdered earlier today. Shortly after she got home." I pointed to the photocopy she was holding. "And she had the original of that list in her filing cabinet."

"*What?*" She gaped at me. "*Dolly?*" She stared down at the list, her mouth still open and her eyes wide. She looked like she might actually laugh at the absurdity of it. "But that's ridiculous."

"It was she who put the list in my pocket, Senator, obviously wanting to protect her employer. But that raises some questions."

"Why didn't she show it directly to me?"

Gallin answered. "That, sure, but she probably assumed you would be irresponsible and dismiss it, the way you did when Mason brought it to your attention. A more interesting question is, where did she get hold of the list? She had the *original* in her apartment. And how did she know to give it to Mason, or where he would be that morning? That is information very, very few people have access to."

Senator Troy was frowning hard. Eventually she said, "I'm sorry, I feel as though I had just stepped through the looking glass. Dolly is—*was*—a very simple, rather naïve girl who was trying to start a career as a PA in DC, and I was trying to give her a hand. The notion that she was somehow involved in cloak and dagger activities involving international assassinations—"

Gallin cut her short. "It is not a notion, Senator. She's

dead. So is Paul Hirschfield. And it was Dolly who placed the list with Paul's name on it in Mason's pocket."

"I am sorry. I can't be of any more help to you than this. I am stunned. The whole thing seems to me totally unreal."

I said, "I hope you will now at least take the need for security more seriously. We'd like to have a couple of agents watching the house and..." I trailed off because my phone had started to ring. "Excuse me."

I stood and walked away toward the desk and stood looking out of the three tall windows. Lovelock's dark brown voice oozed.

"Message from the chief. Costello is here in DC. The chief spoke to him and he has agreed to have a couple of agents sit in his apartment with him and play poker till this is all over."

"Good, but put out the word he's going back to New York and have his apartment watched. What about Reed?"

"He's in LA. According to his wife he went out this morning for a meeting about strategy and funding and he ain't come back. Said he was staying over with some billionaire called George Malkin."

"Not good."

"That's what the chief thinks. He has a couple of teams on the way to the senator's house. One indoors, one outdoors. As soon as they get there, you and your girlfriend head for the airport. The Gulfstream is gassed and ready to go."

"Ten-four." I hung up and turned to Helen Troy. "Senator, we have two teams on their way. I am not asking, I am telling you. One team stays outside and watches the property. The other stays inside and protects you and your family. I do not want any argument from you. Is that understood?"

"I don't appreciate your tone, Mr. Mason."

"I don't care, Senator. I don't need your appreciation. I need your cooperation. I need you and your family to stay safe. Is there anyone else in the house who can provide protection?"

"My driver. He is pretty intimidating. That's why I employed him."

"OK, you keep him by you at all times."

She hesitated. "What about you? Have you got any leads? What happens next?"

"We have to go," I told her. "But I need you to think real hard, and call me the minute you think of anything, however small or absurd it may seem. The question is, how did Dolly get a hold of that list? Who gave it to her? And who told her, ahead of her taking the day off, where I was going to be this morning, so she could slip me the list?"

"I promise, I'll give it some thought and contact you if I think of something. I'll call Jerry—"

I cut across her. "Jerry?"

She gave a small laugh. "Don't worry. I mean Jerry Feynman, he is the president's advisor on national security. Surely I can speak to him!"

I sighed and said ambiguously, "I'm not sure why you'd want to, but if you think it'll help, go ahead. He'll probably tell you it's a hoax."

Gallin stood, frowning. "Did Dolly have contact with Mr. Feynman?"

"What can you mean?"

"It's a pretty simple question, Senator. Did your

personal assistant have contact with the Presidential Advisor of National Security? Privately. As friends, lovers, or in any other configuration? People are dying, Senator Troy."

She made an effort to conceal her distaste and said, "I don't know. I have no idea. I didn't pry into her private life."

"OK." I ran my fingers through my hair, feeling suddenly we were wasting time. "Please stay in touch. Anything, however trivial, let us know."

NINE

I tossed her the keys and told her "You drive," because I knew the way she drove we'd break the light barrier and probably get to the airport before we actually left the senator's house. Aside from that I needed to think.

Gallin gave a disturbing gurgle as the six-hundred-horse-power V12 growled into life, and I think we might have done a wheelie going out of the gate. Once we had settled into a sedate hundred miles per hour I said, "This is like those tabletop jigsaw puzzles, where you need to find the corners before you can make any sense of it."

"So what corners do you think you have already?" I tried to visualize it in my head, but Gallin kept talking. "I keep asking myself, who the hell did he call from a burner? He's the chief intelligence officer at the embassy, for Christ's sake. You can't make more secure calls than the calls you can make from the Israeli Embassy. So why the hell does he go out and buy a burner? Who's he calling? He's calling somebody the embassy shouldn't know about?"

She glanced at me, like I'd have the answer. "That seems to be the inescapable conclusion," I said. "With a bit of luck we'll know tonight."

Streetlamps flashed by, and lonely houses with sleeping cars out front.

"That's one corner. Here's another one. He was gone from the embassy three hours before we found him. In that time he bought a disposable cell, called somebody on it, and within an hour and a half after that he was murdered." I grunted because I didn't like it as a corner. The sky maybe, or grass. But she had her foot on the gas and there was no stopping her. "Because he was killed by the person he called."

"You didn't do a lot of jigsaws, did you, when you were a kid?"

"Not really."

"The corners are indisputable facts. You can't argue or speculate about them. They are the corners."

"So?"

"So we know he had a burner and we know he made a call, but we can only speculate that it was this afternoon, and that the person he called killed him."

She grinned at me as we streaked past the impenetrable shadows of Scott's Run Nature Preserve. "But you know I'm right, don't you?" she said. "Eh? Go on, admit it."

———

MEANTIME, while we were hurtling south in the Mk4 Roadster, Senator Helen Troy was sitting at her lonely walnut desk with the three tall, narrow, dark windows towering behind her. She was staring at the antique, Bakelite telephone on her desk. Eventually she reached for it in a rapid movement, not so much decisive as seizing a moment before it was too late. She pressed the scrambler button and dialed.

It was answered after a couple of rings.

"Yeah?"

"Did you hear about Paul?"

"Is this secure?"

"Of course."

"I'm just getting it now. Who's been sitting on this? The Company didn't have it, nor the Feds. So who had this?"

She knit her brows. "The Pentagon. An office in the Pentagon. Intelligence Networks?"

He sighed. "I might have known. Why'd they go to you? What have you got with Paul?"

"Nothing, but it seems his name was on a list. My name was on the same list."

"Holly shit, Helen! Have you got security?"

"Yes, I have four men like Godzilla's next of kin shambling around the house. Two outside and two inside. I think they are Secret Service."

"OK. Who went to see you, Mason?"

"Yes. Do you know him?"

"Our paths have crossed. He's an arrogant prick."

She was quiet for a moment, then, "He was with another agent, Captain Gallin. Do you know her?"

"A woman? No. Is she Israeli?"

"She had a British accent. She asked if you and Dolly

knew each other, or were close..." She paused, waiting for him to say something. He didn't. "Were you?"

"Come on, Helen! Of course not! She was your secretary, for Christ's sake!"

"You gave her a ride home a couple of times. Did she invite you in for a drink?"

"Helen, stop it. I give lots of people rides..."

"Do you? I don't think you do." Then her voice changed, relented, "I wish you could be here tonight."

"Me too, sugar. But you know how it is. We both have our careers to think of. Especially you. We need to wait till this administration is over. Then things will be different."

"Yeah, OK. So maybe bump into you tomorrow?"

"Yeah, I'll try and find an excuse to have a meeting or something. You'll have to remind me what committees you're on. And keep that imagination of yours under control."

"OK, Jerry, we'll try and catch up tomorrow."

"Sure thing."

"Love you."

"Love you back, baby."

———

SOME HOURS earlier George had engaged the engines of his seventy-foot yacht, turned her prow toward Japan, put her on automatic pilot. From the bridge, he could see Senator Jim Reed luxuriating in the crystalline, turquoise water of the pool. At a table beside the water, in the shade of a blue and white parasol, sat Karen, demure in her light cotton dress. She had a straw hat on her head with a long, crimson ribbon tied around it. She was watching Senator Reid intently as he did lengths. Every so often he would submerge himself, surface and laugh for no apparent reason, and Karen would laugh with him.

George trotted down the stairs, crossed through the saloon and emerged onto the deck. He pulled out a chair and sat beside Karen.

"Why don't you," he said to her, "go and make the senator your special party cocktail. Shelly says she's feeling better. She got a little too much sun this morning. She'll be up in a moment. Then you can change into your bikini and you can both join Jim in the pool and help him drink his cocktail."

Jim laughed again. "Now you are talking my language, George."

Karen stood and made her way inside. George said, "You know, George, I think we can do great things together. You could be one of those presidents, like Roosevelt, Kennedy, Lincoln, where there is a before and an after."

"Well, I have a vision, George. I see a new America, more mature and sophisticated, above all I see—"

"The key, Jim, is America's relationship with Russia. After all, who is the real enemy of the USA? Russia? Not so! It is the European Union, with its protectionism and outdated Soviet ideas about central planning."

Jim waved his arms and legs under the water. "That has always been my view, George."

"Ah! Here is Karen with your cocktail. This, you will enjoy!"

Jim swam to the edge of the pool and Karen hunkered down and smiled at him as he took the drink.

"Now," said George, "that right there is called the Kiss of the Black Widow!" He laughed out loud. "So you can get some idea of what it does to you!" He laughed again. "Karen, honey, while Jim tastes your Kiss of Death, why don't you run along, tell Shelly to get her ass in gear, slip into a topless bikini and have a little swim with Jim. I think he's feeling lonesome."

Karen spoke quietly to Jim. "Try it, I really want you to like it."

He sipped it and his eyes lit up. "Man, that is good!"

"Finish it for me," she said, "and I'll make us another. We can share it."

He drained the glass and watched her hurry away. George observed him quietly for thirty seconds while Jim just stood there, shoulder high in the water, not moving. Finally George said, "You OK there, Jim?"

Jim looked at him and nodded. "Yeah, just."

"Maybe you got too much sun. Here, let me help you out. Sit in the shade for a while, Karen will look after you."

He reached down and gave Jim his hand. Jim climbed the steps with difficulty, saying, "I don't seem to be..."

"That's OK, Jim, don't worry about it. You just lie there on the deck, in the shade." He eased him down until he was lying flat on his back. His eyes were darting from side to side and his tongue was darting between his lips. Noises emerged as he tried to speak, but he couldn't make coherent sounds. His eyes pleaded with George. George nodded. "It's a synthetic, fast-acting curare, known in the trade as a muscular blocker. It paralyzes you, but you remain perfectly conscious. Don't worry. The effect wears off after about an hour."

He saw Jim's eyes look past him and turned. Steve had changed out of his dress and wiped off his makeup, and he had removed his wig. He was now in jeans and a T-shirt, and staring with no emotion at all at the prone man on the deck. In his hands he had a large sheet and a roll of gaffer tape.

Jim's breathing became ragged. He could feel his heart pounding hard and knew that his accelerated pulse would only distribute the poison more quickly.

Steve stood over him. "I'm a boy," he said, "you disgusting pervert. You have a wife at home, and kids, and all you want to do is sleep with boys. You disgusting old pervert. Old men like you should die."

He saw Steve flick his arms out and a moment later he was covered by the soft, white sheet. Then he felt hands under him and he was rolled over and over, and the sheet was pulled tight. He tried to scream but his throat only made a tragic croaking sound.

Then he heard the ripping sound of the gaffer tape as it went first around his ankles, then around his legs and finally around his arms and his body. The last thing was the cord tied around his ankles, tied tight so that it bit into his flesh, and the clang of heavy metal weight.

Then he was being moved, dragged and maneuvered across the deck. He wept, cried out and screamed, all in total, immobile silence. And suddenly he felt the edge of the deck scraping his back and next thing he was in midair.

For a few seconds he was suspended in utter stillness, and then he hit the ocean. The salt water seeped rapidly through the linen and saturated him as he sank rapidly, feet first toward the depths. The water penetrated his mouth and his nose and for a few seconds he experienced terror at a level of sheer hysteria. Panic demands you do something, but when there is nothing you can do, you go beyond despair.

At that moment he might have told Jean-Paul Sartre that hell was not, in fact, other people, as he had said. Hell was being paralyzed, strapped into a weighted sheet, sinking underwater and unable even to scream. He might have told him also, as water violently invaded his lungs and killed him, that life does not begin after despair.

They spent the next few hours on the yacht, and returned to Malibu at around six PM, as the shadow of the pier was stretching long and black across the copper water. The Bentley was there waiting for them and they drove back to the huge, palatial house in silence. They did not speak on the way. Steve never spoke unless he had to, and George deplored violence, and killing always made him feel depressed.

At the circle, where Poseidon was spitting water at the dolphin, Steve got out and waited while George drove to the garage. There he abandoned the Bentley and emerged with a nasty, orange Nissan Sentra. He parked it beside Steve and got out, handed the key to Steve and said, "Leave it at the airport. You will find a ticket to New York and new papers in the glove compartment."

Steve nodded and took the keys. He climbed behind the wheel, a small ugly soul in a small ugly car, and slammed it shut. He opened the window and leaned out, with his arm on the door.

"Goodbye, George. You live well, serving Mother Russia, but such a rich lifestyle, caviar, lobster, steak, wine, cognac..." He trailed off and shook his head. "It's a recipe for a heart attack." He saw the expression on the older man's face and laughed. "Don't worry, George, I have not killed you while you were not looking. How could I? I was never here."

George watched the car slide away into the dark. The two red, demonic eyes of its rear lights watched him from the blackness for a good while after Steve had gone. Finally he shuddered, thanked heavens the nasty young man had gone, and went inside to order a handsome dinner from his chef.

While it was being prepared he made a call to Moscow. The woman's voice was as dry, shriveled and unpleasant as her face had been on the only occasion he had ever met her.

"Report."

"Colonel, the target is dead. His car is parked outside a strip club in Los Angeles. The..." He hesitated a moment. "The asset has left for New York. Colonel, may I speak freely."

"That depends on what you are going to say, Malkin."

"I think this young man is very dangerous."

"Yes, Malkin, that is why we use him."

"He is unpredictable, Colonel, I do not trust him."

"You do not need to predict him, Malkin, and you do not need to trust him. Just pray that he never comes to visit you again."

"Yes, Colonel. You know my loyalty is absolute."

"I know nothing. In the next days maybe the authorities will come looking for Reed. He left yesterday evening. That was the last you saw of him."

"Yes, Colonel. As you say, Colonel."

She hung up and George went to pour himself a large cognac. He drained it at one pull and poured another. He put Wagner's *Der Ring des Nibelungen* on the CD player and sat in his favorite armchair to listen and savor the cognac, and thank whatever gods there be that it was over, and that unpleasant boy was gone.

Meanwhile, down in the kitchen, Gaston, George's master chef, was preparing a superb *boeuf bourguignon*. Gaston had always known, because his mother had told him from as far back as he could remember, that the secret to the perfect *boeuf bourguignon* was enough black pepper. You must put in what you estimate to be the perfect amount, and then a little more. Why? Because the pork lardoons which are essential to make the beef tender, will *steal* the pepper. But the beef *loves* the pepper, so we must add a little extra for the beef. That, he told himself as he sprinkled in a hefty dose of black pepper, and of course *never* to use cooking wine. No, for a good *boeuf bourguignon*, we must use a good wine.

Would you drink cooking wine? No! So why then would you cook with it?

He tasted the stew with his wooden spoon, narrowed his eyes and sprinkled in a little more flaked sea salt, tasted it again and added another dash of black pepper.

What his exquisite palate had probably detected, if he had but known it, was the large quantity of dried, powdered aconite that Steve had added to the black pepper. It would do nothing for the beef stew. It was virtually tasteless and would be almost undetectable in the food, as indeed it would be undetectable in George's blood analysis at the autopsy, if they ever bothered to do one. Because the aconite would provoke a massive heart attack, but, as Steve had warned George just before he left, the way he lived, with his massive cholesterol-rich meals and his wine and spirits, who would question a heart attack? No one. On the contrary, they would expect it.

TEN

WE TOUCHED DOWN IN LA AT ONE THIRTY AM after a three-and-a-half-hour flight where we must have been cruising at over seven hundred miles per hour. At two AM we picked up a Chevy Malibu in the parking lot and headed out directly for George Malkin's country house in East Malibu.

I let Gallin drive because it made her happy and I still needed to think. We took Lincoln Boulevard past Marina del Rey toward Santa Monica, where we cut down to Dog Town and the Pacific Coast Highway. The only clue to the fact that we were entering the small hours was the fact that the sky was dark, and the digital clock on the dash said it was two in the morning. Otherwise the sidewalks were full of people in Bermudas and noisy shirts, the floodlit roads were busy with traffic, and there was that same sense of perpetual holiday that permeates large parts of Los Angeles all year round.

As we hit the coast she accelerated and we opened the

windows to let the sea breeze batter us. Out in the blackness of the ocean you could see the faintly luminous glow of the foam on the breakers, and the distant lights of a couple of ships.

Gallin said, suddenly, "Why would the Presidential Advisor on National Security be in possession of a hit list composed of presidential candidates—"

"Candidates for nomination."

"Candidates for nomination, party supporters, an Israeli security officer and three enemies of the Russian state?"

"That is not so hard to answer. A man in his position can come by that kind of document in any number of ways. The CIA might have given it to him, or the NSA. The big question would be, why did he give it to Dolly?"

She frowned at me. A cluster of lights at the Santa Monica Canyon washed over her face.

"You say that like you know he did."

I shrugged. "No, but I am struggling to find another way she got a hold of it."

She pulled up at a set of lights, resting her wrist on the wheel in front of her. "Yeah, I know," she said absently. "But even assuming Jerry Feynman gave her the list, what made him do that? Why not warn Helen directly? And why the hell would he tell Dolly to slip you the list on a train?"

"No." I shook my head. "That makes no sense. Unless…"

"Unless he is involved in something and wants out."

"That is what I was going to say, yes."

She grinned as she pulled away from the lights. "But I got there first. OK, let's explore that. Unknown person wants the people on those lists dead."

"OK, that's a corner."

"Yeah, the fact that an annex of the list holds three enemies of the Russian state, suggests that it might be a Russian list—"

"Maybe—"

"He *was* more interested in saving the stock market than finding the cases."

"Let's leave it at maybe. He's a politician. They have no moral compass."

"OK, whatever. So they bring pressure to bear on Jerry to have the list executed, but he doesn't like it. Maybe he doesn't believe they can pull it off, or he's afraid he'll become the fall guy when it's all over—"

"He's seen what happened to Maria and Peter..."

"Right, and he thinks he might go the same way. So he gets Dolly to slip you the list, hoping you'll pull his nuts out of the fire for him, when the time comes."

"Which means we have to assume Jerry is in the pay of the Russians. I don't like the man, but we actually have no evidence to support that belief."

"Except he is the only person we know of who was both in a position to have that kind of intel *and* pass it to Dolly."

I thought about it, nodded and said, "Thin."

"Thin." Then she gave a small twitch of her head and said, "Let's see what Reed and Costello have to say about him."

We came eventually to Carbon Beach. It was silent and still. The few establishments there were were closed and had their lights turned off, and only the streetlamps illuminated the empty road. We turned onto a concrete track and immediately began to climb. The road twisted and wound, following the contours of the canyon and the hills that flanked it, as it grew ever deeper and darker.

Pretty soon the only light was the haze that rose up from beyond the black humps we'd left behind us, and the occasional solitary bulbs that illuminated the walled gardens of the scattered houses, cloistered among whispering trees.

The last house on the track was the one we were looking for. It was as enormous and palatial as it was grotesque, and stood protected behind a high wall and an electronic, steel gate. There were no immediate signs of life, but we rang and hammered for a couple of minutes and eventually a tired voice came over the intercom.

"Who is it? We did not order nothing."

"We are federal agents, sir. We need to talk to Senator James Reed."

"He is not here. He gone."

"Then we need to talk to Mr. George Malkin. Can you open the door and talk to us please, sir?"

There was a silence long enough to count slowly to ten. Then a heavy sigh that was more than half groan, and the steel door began to roll back.

We moved into a driveway that was flanked by gardens and came to a grotesque, imitation classical fountain showing Poseidon spouting water from his mouth and hitting a bottlenose dolphin in the eye. The house itself was oddly reminiscent of the Kremlin and gave you the feeling all the roofs were made of meringue. We parked outside the front door and by the time we'd climbed out and crossed the gardens to the porch, the door had opened, revealing a sad man in blue and white pajamas and a dressing gown.

His first words were, "May I see some identification, please?"

I showed him my card and pointed at Gallin with my thumb. "This is my partner, Captain Aila Gallin."

She flashed her Mossad badge at him too fast for him to see what it said and he handed me back my card.

"Please come in."

He led us through the entrance hall and down a passage to a large kitchen where he had a small TV playing on an ancient dresser. He had a place set for himself at a heavy pine table with the remains of a beef stew, which was still rich in the air, a baguette and half a bottle of decent claret. He switched off the TV and gestured to us to sit down. His accent when he spoke was French...

"Please, may I offer you some wine? Some cognac? You have dined already at this time, I assume."

"That's kind of you. We actually need to see Senator Jim Reed or George Malkin."

He closed his eyes and shook his head, muttering, "*Ce n'est pas possible!* It is not possible. *M. le sénateur* he left, he did not even 'ave dinner. I prepare a splendid *lapin a la cocotte* but he does not stay. He leaves and so I have to freeze the rabbit, or throw it away."

Gallin was going up and down on her toes. I could sense she was getting antsy. We were both hungry and tired. She said, "So, he just left with no explanation?"

"*Bon!* Nobody explain nothing to me. I am just the chef! But he go. Nobody say to me, 'Eh, Gascon! *M. le sénateur* he no stay for dinner.' No, he just go."

I asked him, "What about George Malkin?"

He hunched his shoulders and waved his hands around while spluttering the way only the French know how. "*Eh bien! Il est mort!* Eating... eating my..." He gestured at the table with both hands, in outrage. "My *boeuf bourguignon!* 'Ow?" He said it three times, still gesturing at the table, his cheeks flushed red, "'Ow? 'Ow? 'Ow can a man die of eating my *boeuf bourguignon?*"

I held up a hand. "Wait. You are telling me that Senator James Reed disappeared and Mr. Malkin died, all in the same day?"

"Yes! And the girl or boy, *hermaphrodite*, also! I tell the police and the doctor, there is nothing wrong with my stew! But the doctor he say, 'No, no, is not your stew. Is just an 'art attack.'"

I pulled out a chair and sat. We had all been standing up until that point. Now he grabbed a couple of tumblers and gave us a glass of wine each. We sat, knocked glasses and drank. It was good wine.

"Gascon?" I asked. He nodded. "Gascon, have you still got the *boeuf bourguignon* and the ingredients?"

He shook his head. "No. I threw everything away. I tell them, you take the ingredients! You check! You see if I have used anything but the very best ingredients! But they tell me 'No, no! You don't worry!' So I throw everything out. Everything away. The meat, the vegetables, the herbs, the spices, everything! My food does not make an 'art attack in my employer! Eh?"

I smiled and tapped my nose. "If the smell is anything to go by, I believe you!"

"*Alors!*" He spread his hands.

"How long have you worked for Mr. Malkin, Gascon?"

"Only three months, not more."

Gallin, reading my thoughts, asked, "Always in this house?"

"He rent this house, and he employ staff for the house. He say, if he likes it he will buy it."

"Did he do much entertaining? Did he have a lot of visitors?"

"*Eh bien!* He has visitors. Sometimes they come and I do not 'ave to cook. Sometimes they come and I 'ave to cook." He arched an eyebrow and gave what you could only describe as a knowing smile.

Gallin said, "The people you had to cook for were special, more important, clients?"

"Aha, I tell you. The people for whom I 'ad not to cook, all were Russian. *Mais,* the people for whom I cook, all were American! What do you think of this!"

"That is very interesting."

He started counting them out on his fingers. "Senators, governors, *les industriels!* Always the very important people. The people of *influence!*"

"And the Russians?"

"*Mais oui!* Also! But no parties, no dinners, no, no!"

"So what happens to you now, Gaston?"

"I know not! Tomorrow I suppose I must leave."

I gave him my card. "Whatever happens, call me and let me know, will you?"

"Of course!"

"Thanks for the wine." I went to stand, but hesitated, frowning. "You said something about an hermaphrodite?"

"*Ouis!* Also gone! Impossible to tell if it was a man or a

woman! Well," he shrugged and waved his hands around, "a man it was not! Whatever else it was, it was not a man! Sometimes dressed like a boy, sometimes like a girl. Bizarre!"

"Who was this?" I asked. "A friend of Malkin's?"

"*Bien sur!* He brings him home, I have to feed him. He does not comment on my food! *C'est une pute!* He is an 'ore! He dress like a girl for *M. le sénateur*, then he is disappear, like *M. le sénateur!* Maybe they go together. I do not know."

Gallin asked, "Was this person ever in the kitchen?"

He looked surprised. "Yes, I am discussing the menu with M. Malkin, and when I come back to the kitchen, he is going around, like he is in his own house. I tell him, 'Go from my kitchen!' He just make me the smile and leave."

I pulled my cell and called Nero.

"What the devil do you want? Do you know what time it is?"

"Yes sir, but we need to act with speed and you are going to make this happen much faster than I can."

"Make what happen?"

"George Malkin has been poisoned with aconite. It will not normally show up in an autopsy unless they are looking for it. You need to pull strings and make them look for aconite in George Malkin's blood."

"Goddammit! What about Reed?"

"Disappeared. I'll report later, sir."

He hung up and I looked at Gascon. "It was very fortunate for you, Gascon, that you threw away the ingredients you used for that meal. Did you eat any of it?"

"No, no! Just taste on the spoon. But I did not kill M. Malkin! Why would I...?"

Gallin answered him, "Of course you didn't. While you

were talking to George Malkin, the killer came into the kitchen and poisoned your ingredients."

"But *why?*"

She shook her head and smiled. "Best you don't know. George Malkin was involved with some bad people, Gascon. The less you know, the better. Can you describe this person for us?"

He tried, but we didn't get much. He did a lot of French shrugging and spreading his hands, pulling his mouth down at the corners. When he dressed as a man he looked like "*Un garçon homosexuel,*" but when he was dressed as a girl he was "*Une fille!* You cannot tell. Still, I do not know if it is a boy or a girl or both!"

The face was impossible to describe. Not unpleasant, but, "Something in the eyes, no feeling, just watching you, watching all the time; and quiet."

I took what details I could and sent them to Lovelock without much hope she would make anything of them. I made Gascon promise he would go and see a doctor, and by the time we stepped out to the drive, the sky was turning gray over the San Gabriel mountains. I leaned on the roof of the car, aware of the exhaustion in my back and my legs. I had been almost forty-eight hours without sleep. Gallin leaned on the far side and smiled at me.

"Are we tired and hungry?"

"More than words can express, and we are still playing catch-up. This bastard is already on his way either to New York or back to DC. He is working through the list in any order he pleases, to keep us running after him and bumping into ourselves going the other way."

"At least we have something like a description."

I grunted and smiled back at her. "He looks like air, except when he's wet. Then he looks like water."

"He is the original invisible man. Or woman. He is going to be hard to find."

I climbed in the car and she got behind the wheel. "Except," I said, "he is not the classic gray man. There is something unsettling about this person. You don't notice him until you look at him, and then..."

She fired up the engine. "Come on. We need to decide whether to see Reed's wife or chase this creep to New York or DC. Let's go find a motel and get a few hours' sleep. If you're lucky I'll give you a massage before you go to sleep?"

I stared at her. "Seriously?"

"Mm-hmm, but you have to give me one back."

"I promise."

I grabbed my phone and called Nero again. He answered immediately with:

"They are looking for traces of aconite even now as we speak."

"That's fantastic, sir. Thank you. Sir, I need you to debrief me right now. Because very shortly I am going to go to sleep."

"Good grief, Alex. Really?"

"Yes, sir. Our assassin is on his way to New York, or DC, he is about five-two and apparently sexless."

"Sexless?"

"Yes, sir." I glanced at Gallin, who was laughing quietly. I repeated, "Sexless. He can seem to be male or female..."

Two minutes later I had finished my debriefing. I hung up and smiled nicely at Gallin.

"You know what? We are both exhausted and hungry.

Screw the motel. Let's have four or five hours at the Ritz-Carlton. It's twenty minutes from LAX. We'll get room service, some champagne, two dozen oysters, have a soak in a tub, I'll give you a massage, you give me a massage, and by midday tomorrow we'll be good as new. What do you say?"

She gave me a naughty smile back and said, "OK."

ELEVEN

Nero had not slept that night either. And as he hung up his telephone there was a knock at the door, it opened and a spotty young man in a dirty T-shirt came in, accompanied by a very clean, spruce young man in a blue shirt that looked freshly ironed. These were Graham and Navreet. They were accompanied by Ted, the head of the Forensic Department. Nero looked at his watch. It was seven AM and he was badly in need of coffee, croissants, smoked Norwegian salmon, a shower and several hours' deep sleep.

He gestured at the chairs opposite him and said, "Lovelock, lots of coffee please, and hot buttered croissants." Then he turned to his guests. "Navreet, Graham, Ted. I believe you have information for me. Navreet, Graham, why don't you go first. Why are these people on a list together?"

Graham spoke while fingering a spot on his unshaven cheek. "Sir, our initial impression seems to have been born out by events. We have two groups of people—" Navreet had started nodding, watching Nero. Graham continued. "We can classify these two groups as Group A and Group B."

As though by silent agreement Navreet started talking and Graham started nodding. "We tried at first to define each group by the people within it, but we kept running across inconsistencies. Group A is eighty-four percent American, and sixteen percent Israeli. Those percentages hold as eighty-four percent affiliated to that political party, and sixteen percent not affiliated. However, the non-affiliated non-American, was sympathetic to that party."

"Is this going somewhere?"

Graham answered. "Yes, sir, we can define List A as being entirely concerned with the power struggle within that political party."

Nero grunted, "Hm, very well, and?"

Navreet spoke, "List B—Group B—seems on the face of it to be incongruent with List A. It is sixty-six percent Russian and thirty-three percent American, but one hundred percent concerned with the suitcase bombs. So our next challenge was to define why the two lists were stapled together."

"And?"

Graham leaned forward with his elbows on his knees. "We decided that List B, when taken alone, had an integrity and a coherence that was missing in List A. There were no loose, background percentages or fractions. So we decided, as a thought experiment, that List A must fit into List B. Which meant we had to find connections between the seven people on List A and the suitcase bombs."

Nero sat forward, scowling. "*And...?*"

The door opened and Lovelock came in with a large tray

laden with coffee and croissants. Nero directed his scowl at her and growled, "Put it down and go, woman!"

Graham reached for a croissant while Ted poured coffee and Navreet spoke.

"So far the links we have found are tenuous, but they are there, and our good friend, Ted," he offered Ted a big grin, "has been most helpful in establishing those connections."

"Get on with it, man!"

"Yes, sir. Senator Reed was extremely vocal in condemning Russia over the suitcases, and expressing the view that the so-called REDS terrorist organization was merely a front for Putin's illegal activities. He was vocal in condemning Russia over that and the Ukraine war and in calling for severe sanctions."

Graham cleared his throat and sipped coffee while Navreet reached for a croissant.

"Senator Costello had a number of ties with Russian companies. He had invested quite extensively in Russian stock and notably Russian oil. He was notably muted when calling for sanctions. However, when it emerged that the device had been found and that two Russian agents were responsible, he started cutting his ties like they were contaminated with strontium." He allowed himself a brief laugh. "He now advocates cutting ties with Russia and strengthening ties with the Arabs."

Navreet spoke with his mouth full. "With Priti Anand and Johannes de Jong we find the same story. Both of them had invested heavily in Russia. When the war broke out and then the suitcase crisis happened, they were both vocal in saying that sanctions were not the way forward, give the Russians the Donbas, why did Ukraine need to be part of

NATO, et cetera. They also stated publicly several times that the suitcases were just a hoax. When the nuclear device was found in New York, they changed their tune and became advocates of cutting ties with Russia and strengthening ties with Saudi and the other Arab oil producers, such as Iran."

Nero sagged back in his chair and stared at the coffee pot. "How could I have missed this?" He reached for his cup and drained it, handing it absently to Ted who refilled it. "And here of course is the relevance of Colonel Hirschfield. He could see that the long-term effect of American dependence on Arab oil could be disastrous for Israel." He frowned at his coffee and then at Navreet. "But no, that puts him at odds with the others on the list."

Navreet nodded. "Apparently so, until you dig a little deeper. The third candidate is Helen Mila Troy."

"Mila?"

"Her grandparents were Russian Jews, Talman, and escaped from Russia at the end of World War Two. They established themselves in the USA and did OK. It seems they were distant cousins of Hirschfield's and got to know each other through various activities and foundations and stuff. When Paul Hirschfield moved to the States they hooked up and he became like a mentor for young Helen. During the start of the Ukraine war and during the suitcase crisis, Colonel Hirschfield was outspoken about coming down hard on Russia. Senator Troy echoed his demands. Colonel Hirschfield also pointed out Russia's willingness to use Islamic troops against the Ukrainians and called Russia and the Arab states an unholy alliance. Troy has since taken a more neutral stance—she's obviously wondering where her oil is going to come from if she ever makes it to president—but that connects her and Colonel Hirschfield with Russia and with everybody else on both lists."

Nero's cheeks were flushed with barely suppressed rage. "Are you telling me this is a punitive hit list from the Kremlin, directed at American nationals and Congressmen?"

Navreet and Graham nodded together. "Yes, sir."

"There are a couple of other points, sir." It was Ted; Nero looked at him with bulging eyes. "More?"

"Captain Mason noticed that Colonel Hirschfield had a disposable cell in his pocket and asked us to have a look at it. When we did we found that the SIM card had been removed so we could not trace any calls. However, Captain Mason had observed that only some of the numbers had been smudged." Seeing Nero's frown he explained, "These are what are known as Dumb Phones for seniors, and they have buttons instead of a touch screen."

"And he observed that some of the buttons had been pressed."

"And asked us to make an analysis of those numbers and try to come up with whom he had called."

"And?"

Ted nodded a few times before answering. "It was a number at the White House, sir. It was Jerry Feynman's private office at the White House."

Nero closed his eyes and sank back in his huge chair.

Ted watched him uneasily for a moment. "We were able to trace the call and found that it was made within little more than an hour of the colonel's presumed time of death. But there is a little more..."

Nero opened his eyes, grabbed his phone and dialed.

WE SIGNED in at the Ritz-Carlton, told them to send up a bottle of very cold Dom Pérignon and two dozen oysters, and made our weary way up in the elevator, grinning at each other like schoolkids. As I unlocked the door Gallin said, "I bagsie the bath first."

I let her in, frowning. "Bagsie?"

"Stake my claim."

"Oh." I closed the door and she made for the bathroom, kicking off her shoes. "That's fine. I thought maybe I could feed you champagne and oysters while you bathe, and massage your poor back."

She poked her head out of the bathroom and smiled, but didn't say anything. Then withdrew it again. I heard the water start to run in the bath and saw her light cotton dress float to the floor through the crack in the door. I pulled off my jacket, crunched my spine and my shoulders and, looking out at the pre-dawn skyline told myself I was tired, but not that tired.

There was a tap at the door and I went and opened it. A waiter wheeled in a trolley with an ice bucket, two chilled champagne flutes, a silver platter of oysters and a red rose. I gave the waiter twenty bucks and shooed him away. I closed the door behind him and trotted back to the trolley where I opened the champagne with a loud pop and heard a giggle from the bathroom, followed by, "I'm ready!"

I poured two glasses, and popped the rose into one of them, then eased open the door. Gallin was in the bath, conveniently covered with suds. She had her hair tied in a knot exposing the back of her neck, and she grinned at me in the mirror and winked.

"Is that rose for me?"

"Who else?"

I took it out and put it in a tooth mug, then handed her the glass. I sat on the toilet and we touched glasses. She giggled as we drank.

"I could get used to this side of Alex Mason."

"Yeah? Wait till I refill your glass and bring you the oysters."

I wheeled in the trolley and put it beside the bath. She swallowed an oyster while I refilled her glass. She made a disturbingly nice noise and said, "I was promised a back massage."

"And by Jove you'll get one. Just as soon as I have had this oyster and rolled up my sleeves."

I did both, took a pull on my champagne and sat behind her at the end of the bath. Suddenly she wasn't giggling anymore. I could see her eyes closed in the mirror and as I put my hands on her shoulders she smiled and let out a deep sigh. "Mason, I don't give a damn, this is exactly what I need."

That was when the phone rang.

"Don't even think about answering it!"

It was on the trolley and I glanced at the screen. "It's Nero."

"Son of a *bitch!*"

I picked up the phone and tried to sound as if I had been asleep. "Sir...?"

"I don't care how tired you are! Stop whatever you are

doing and get here now! You can sleep on the plane! Now, Alex! Hang up and do it now!"

I hung up and we sat staring at each other in the mirror. After a moment she drained her glass and, staring at it, she said sullenly, "You had better not be in here when I get out of the bath."

I nodded and left with the bottle.

––––––––

WE ARRIVED in Nero's office at a little after one PM local time. Nero looked like he hadn't slept for a week, which gave me some dark kind of satisfaction, and Ted was there looking like he was fresh out of a twelve-hour sleep marathon.

Nero's first words were, "I know you're tired and I am sorry. But we need to put an end to this before Moscow decapitates one of the only two parties we have."

We sat and Nero laid both his huge hands on the desk in front of him.

"Let me start by saying that these lists were in no way what we had assumed. These lists are nothing more than an executive *execution* order, a hit list, as you said, Alex, but issued by the Kremlin as punishment against people who have either failed her, or have failed to toe the line."

I frowned hard and started to ask, "Well, how much influence..."

But Nero slammed his palm down on the table and bellowed, *"How dare they! How dare they punish American citizens and American politicians, and Israeli officers, for not dancing to their tune!"*

I went to speak again but he bellowed, "*This man has gone out of his mind! He believes he can send his tendrils in here and turn our congressmen to his will with bribes and threats of murder? We must stop him! And we must stop him today! And punish him for his damned effrontery!*"

"Sir?"

"*What, dammit?*"

"What has happened?"

He held up one thick thumb. "Senator Reed, extremely vocal in condemning Russia over Ukraine and the suitcases, and calling for severe sanctions." He raised his index. "Senator Costello, despite his ties with Russian oil and his reluctance to back sanctions, when it emerged that the device had been found and that Russian agents were responsible, he cut his links and now advocates dumping Russia and strengthening ties with the Arabs." He raised his middle finger.

"Priti Anand and Johannes de Jong had both invested heavily in Russia. They were both vocal in opposing sanctions. They also stated publicly that the suitcases were a hoax. But when you found the nuclear device in New York, they too advocated cutting ties with Russia and strengthening ties with Arab oil producers."

He raised another finger.

"Colonel Hirschfield understood that the long-term effect of American dependence on Arab oil would be disastrous for Israel." He paused and sighed heavily. "He was, it seems, a close family friend and a mentor to Helen Troy. Helen *Mila* Troy. Her family is originally Russian, but under Hirschfield's guidance she too was highly critical of Russia. She has since softened her tone, but Moscow is apparently unforgiving."

"So this is nothing more than a hit list of people who have crossed the Kremlin's interests in the USA?"

"Yes, and that means one thing, Alex, that the Kremlin *expected* cooperation. And *that* means they have been spending money and expect a return! The Kremlin has mined too deep into the Capitol *and* the White House!"

"The White House?"

"Yes indeed! The telephone you spotted in Hirschfield's pocket. It had no SIM card."

"I know sir, he would have destroyed that and thrown it away."

"Shut up, Alex. However, there were smudges on the keys which you helpfully pointed out to Ted. They led to a telephone number in the White House."

"Aha!" I snapped my fingers. "Jerry Feynman!"

Nero gave a massive sigh. He looked at Ted and then at Gallin.

"Yes, Alex," he said, "Jerry Feynman was the last person Colonel Hirschfield called before he died. At his private office at the White House."

I scratched my head and Gallin spoke my thoughts.

"That doesn't make a lot of sense. It should have been Jerry Feynman who bought the burner to call Paul. Why would Paul call Feynman at the White House from a burner?"

Nero growled, "I suggest you go and ask him. Meantime, there is more—"

I interrupted the chief and addressed Ted. "Did you look at incoming calls on his house phone?"

"Not yet. We're working round the clock."

"Prioritize that for me, would you, Ted?"

"You got it. We'll look at that this morning."

"Are you done?" It was Nero.

"Of course, sir."

"Ted tells me they got a hit on the tissue under Dolores Scott's nails. Isaiah Luomo, from the Island of Tonga. Of no known address. He was charged with murder one, and possession of class B drugs with intent to distribute. Somehow his lawyer got him bail and he vanished. We have a BOLO out for him nationwide." He pressed a button on his desk and said, "Lovelock, send Mason and Captain Gallin pictures of Isaiah Luomo, will you?"

A moment later my phone pinged and I looked at the photograph. He must have been six-six crowding seven foot, with shoulders like an overinflated bouncy castle and arms like condoms stuffed with walnuts. I had never seen him before, so I wondered why he seemed familiar. I looked at Nero.

"Anything else?"

"Yes! Go and drag that hideous upstart Feynman from his office and waterboard him until he tells you what he knows!"

"Do you have anyone on him?"

He held my eye and nodded.

TWELVE

I HAD AN OFFICE AT ODIN WHICH I NEVER USED. IT had a computer and a couple of filing cabinets where a secretary I had never met occasionally filed things. I went there now to call Jerry Feynman. My reason for doing that was because I knew his screen would tell him the call was coming from ODIN. That would worry him and I wanted him to worry.

It rang five times before he answered it. Then a voice, on the rude side of curt, said, "Yeah."

"That is one of the signs of a man who knows he has a problem."

His, "*What?*" was an abbreviated, *What the hell are you talking about?*

"Sitting, looking at your phone, watching it ring and wondering whether to answer it. That is a man who knows he has a problem."

"Who is this?"

"Why, Jerry, you're going to hurt my feelings. It's your old buddy from ODIN, Mason, Alex Mason. You remember me, doncha? I'm the one who pulled your nuts out of the fire when you screwed up about the suitcase bombs."

"What do you want, Mason?"

"Well, you being the personal advisor to the president on matters of national security, and me being a man in possession of *a lot* of national security intelligence, I thought maybe you and I could get together over a whiskey or two, and discuss ways in which I could do you a favor."

"What kind of favor?"

"Well, Jerry, I have had my ear to the ground, and I have been listening to the grapevine and I have also been talking to the little birdies, and you know what? They are all saying the same thing: 'Man! That Jerry Feynman sure screwed up!'"

I glanced at Gallin and she nodded. We'd discussed it in the corridor and we had agreed. Now she was telling me, 'Do it.' Feynman said nothing so I pressed him. "I mean, that is the word around town, and that *is* what Paul was talking to you about, right?"

Some might have thought it a long shot. I didn't and neither did Gallin. There were a limited number of things Colonel Paul Hirschfield would have discussed with Jerry Feynman, and ninety-nine point nine percent of those he would have discussed on the embassy phone. That point naught one percent stood a damned good chance of being about his handling of the suitcase affair, because that would have had serious implications for Israel; and *that* stood a good chance of being the reason for his presence on the list.

Either way, long shot or not, it seemed to hit the bull because he cursed under his breath, "*Jesus Christ!*" and then, "What do you know about..."

He trailed off. "Are you sure this is the time and place you want to be having this conversation, Jerry?"

Very softly he said, "What did he tell you?"

"You know what, Jerry? I don't think you are very interested in meeting. I don't think you fully understand what is going on here. I think maybe I should call back in a couple of days. Maybe I'll come and see you in your cell."

Gallin winced. She thought I'd overshot the mark, but my hunch paid off.

"Wait! Keep your panties on. OK, where do you want to meet?"

"Off the Record, half an hour. We'll have a late lunch."

I hung up and grinned at Gallin. She said, "Our boy has a very guilty conscience."

I laughed, "On the other hand, pick a White House employ at random and tell him, 'I'll come and visit you in your cell,' and there's a good chance he'll go pale and offer you money."

"OK, let's go meet him."

TWO MILES across the river Jerry put down his phone and called his secretary. She stepped into his large office and crossed the deep pile blue carpet to his desk. Jerry was staring at the window and she had to say, "Yes, Mr. Feynman?" before he looked at her and frowned.

"When is my next meeting with the president?"

"Tomorrow morning, sir. This afternoon you have—"

"Cancel everything for this afternoon. Something has come up and I have to go out. If anyone calls for me, take their number and tell them I'll get back to them."

He stood, grabbed his jacket and left. Trotting down the stairs he made for the Executive Avenue exit and climbed into his dark blue Range Rover with tinted windows without being seen. He left via the First Infantry Division Monument gate onto 17th Street and turned right. Nobody followed him and he began to relax. As he turned into H Street he called Helen on her private line. She sounded pleased.

"Hey, where are you?"

"Driving. Listen, has Mason been in touch with you?"

"Mason? No, what's going on?"

"He called, said he wants to meet me."

"What about?"

"I don't know. But this guy is dangerous. He said it was something to do with Hirschfield."

"When does he want to meet?"

"Now. At Off the Record. Has he said anything to you about me? Or asked about me?"

"...no...," she said absently, then gave a pretty laugh. "Well, look, I must get on. I am overwhelmed with work today. But call me this afternoon, after five, and we'll have a drink and discuss things."

"You're with someone?"

"Right," and a little more distantly, "Come in, come in, please sit down," then into the phone again, "Call me after five," and she hung up.

He felt a surge of rage. He was the president's personal advisor, goddammit! She should be groveling to talk to him, and instead she was giving him the brush-off! If he did not contain things fast, he was seriously at risk of being cut adrift. In that city, if people caught the faintest whiff that you were in trouble, that you were a victim, your friends disappeared faster than a bowl of punch at an AA convention. He had to keep cool, not contact anybody else, and give Mason whatever the hell it was he wanted. Take the pressure off just long enough so he could fix the problem.

He drove around in circles for a while, and found his mind was doing the same thing. So he headed for the Hay Adams, left his car with the valet parking and made his way down the gray, granite steps under the red awning on H Street, to the plush, red velvet luxury of the Off the Record bar. The lunchtime crowd was thinning out and he found a quiet table in the corner, beneath the caricatures of Jimmy Carter and Bobby Kennedy, who seemed suddenly to be jeering at him. He ordered a Glenfiddich on the rocks, gathered his ugly thoughts about him and settled to wait.

Meanwhile, exactly three thousand and twelve yards from where he was sitting, Helen Mila Troy sat and stared at the empty seats opposite her, beyond the walnut expanse of her desk.

Jerry was a player. Paul had always told her so. "He plays fast and loose. But you know what you need if you are going to play fast and loose in politics?"

She smiled at the memory and felt a deep pang of loss. Every time she had answered the same, "I know you're going to tell me, uncle."

"You need humility, Minnie. Because if you play fast and

loose with arrogance, however good you are, you are going to get burned. And burned in politics is bad news."

Uncle.

He had been more than a mentor. He had been family. The only person in the world she could trust. Now he was gone, like her mother, her father and her husband. All she had left was the bleak winter of her career, to ascend, like the Ice Queen, to the White Castle and become the most powerful woman in the world. Paul had told her, not so long ago, "Don't sell your soul for politics, Minnie Smirnova, it is a poor deal."

Smirnov had been her father's name. He had sold his soul to drag his family out of Russia, and then out of the American gutter. Paul knew that, which was why he used to tell her, "Don't sell your soul."

She had looked at him and loved him, more than his wife ever had, and told him, "I never will."

She drew a deep breath and dragged her mind back to Jerry. What had he done? Paul had never liked Jerry. He attributed Iran's growing power, their defiance of the Joint Comprehensive Plan of Action and the administration's failure to address Iran's nuclear power and her support of anti-Israeli terrorism as a single issue, squarely at Jerry's door. She had always believed he exaggerated. Too many years in international politics had made him paranoid, she used to tell him. "You see everything as a threat to Israel!"

"Minnie! Everything *is* a threat to Israel! You know why I want you to be president?"

"Because you love me?"

"No, that's why I *don't* want you to be president. I want you to be president because none of these idiots understands how much the West needs Israel, and how much Israel needs the USA. Without Israel, the United States and the United Kingdom would collapse overnight. And without the USA, the whole Arab world would march on Israel. Maybe, maybe I can make you understand that."

She understood it. Jerry did not understand it. Jerry saw only two things: Arab oil and Russian investment. Correction. He saw three things, and the third was the amount of money he could make at the back door selling his influence with the president to the highest bidder. He was a short-termist who cared only about feathering his own nest.

And Paul had hinted darkly to her recently. The Mossad was without equal when it came to covert operations and surveillance. Had he caught Jerry with his pants down? Had he caught Jerry doing what he didn't oughta?

Had Jerry found out? She got a flash of the conversation they had had recently over the telephone. He had asked who had been to see her, and whether it was Mason. She had asked if he knew Mason and he had replied that their paths had crossed, and that Mason was an arrogant prick. He was not wrong there. But then she had mentioned that Mason had been with a woman, a Captain Gallin, and had immediately asked if she was Israeli?

Why? It wasn't like the USA was short on Jews. Something like two and a half percent of the population was Jewish, and most of those were on the East Coast. If she'd told him her lawyer was called Bennie Goodman, would he have asked if he was Israeli?

A deep and troubling certainty settled on her. Paul had caught Jerry and was threatening him: Leave the White House of your own free will, or I'll have you thrown out.

．　．　．

AT THAT VERY MOMENT WE, Gallin and I, were approaching H Street along 17ᵗʰ Street NW. Her telephone rang, she arched an eyebrow at the screen and put it on speaker.

"Captain Aila Gallin speaking."

"Captain, this is Senator Troy speaking. Is this a convenient time for you to speak? Are you alone?"

Gallin glanced at me a moment, like she was wondering whether I really existed or not and said, ambiguously, "Yes, sure."

I told myself this was the price people paid for asking two questions at the same time, and turned right into H Street. It was bright and sunny, and had that Georgian, Old-World feel that DC sometimes has, as we cruised slowly past Lafayette Square. Senator Troy was saying, "Forgive me for asking, Captain, but I am afraid I didn't really pay attention yesterday. Am I right in saying that you are from the Mossad?"

She looked at me and raised both eyebrows. "Yes, Senator. We are cooperating with the Pentagon."

"Why?"

Gallin gave a small laugh. "I am sorry, Senator, I can't discuss that with you, and far less on the phone. But I should have thought it was obvious. Paul was attached to the embassy, and the murder took place on embassy property. You can draw your own conclusions. Is there something you need to tell me?"

The senator was quiet for a bit, then, "I have been

thinking about Paul's death. We were very close, as I told you."

"Yes?"

"There are things, things that he said..." She trailed off. "I wonder if you'd be willing to come and see me, alone?"

"Of course. Where and when?"

"Now? At my office? I'm at the Russell Senate Office Buildings."

Gallin glanced at me. I nodded. "I'll be there in ten minutes."

I watched her drive away in my Mk4 and trotted down the steps to the Off the Record. It's a bar I like because it has a kind of understated opulence you would normally associate with the Old World, yet manages to make it feel quintessentially American. But it's a bar I don't frequent, because I don't want the people who go there to become familiar with my face.

I found Jerry sitting in a corner being sneered at by caricatures of Bobby Kennedy and Jimmy Carter. I ordered a Bushmills, straight up and sat opposite him. He observed me without speaking, like he was wishing looks could kill.

"You know why, Jerry, your career in politics must ultimately fail?" He didn't say anything, so I continued. "You got to work in the Oval Office by a mixture of bravado, recklessness and exploiting the stupidity of others." I shrugged. "It's what everybody does in politics. But you, unlike many others, have consistently failed ever to learn anything from your mistakes. Politics is natural selection at work, Jerry. Natural selection requires adaptability, and that means learning from your mistakes. You, sooner rather than later, are going down." I waited. He still said nothing. I said, "Unless, of course, you let me help you."

He made a face of disgust. "At least Paul was honest about it."

"Paul was a very honest man. Paul was everything you are not. Paul gave good advice, and that is why everybody trusted him. You give bad advice which serves only your interest. Paul was loyal and committed to his country and his allies. You are loyal only to yourself. I believe the only person left in Washington who still believes you is the president, and you can be sure somebody is whispering in his ear even now."

He looked into his glass and rattled the ice. "Is this all you've got, Mason? 'Cause I'm getting bored. You want to give me one good reason why I shouldn't tell you to go to hell and walk out the door?"

The waiter brought my Bushmills. I sipped it and set it down, holding his eye the while. "Because," I said, "when you killed Paul, you didn't go through his papers. His murder occurred on Israeli territory, Paul. Which means it is being investigated jointly by ODIN and the Mossad."

"They think I killed him?"

"No, Jerry, we know you paid someone to kill him. And I have received an informal request. In exchange for not causing a scandal that will embarrass the president, you get sent as part of a diplomatic mission to Israel..."

"No."

"You know the Israelis, Jerry. They *really* don't like people killing their heroes. Very Old Testament."

He was shaking his head. "No, no, you have got this all wrong."

I nodded. "Now you are beginning to understand. Start with the phone call you got from Paul just before he died and work your way back. I want everything, and I want to know exactly how the Russians tie in."

He rubbed his face with his hands and stared at Jimmy Carter a moment. Finally he said, "OK, I'll tell you everything."

THIRTEEN

PRITI ANAND SAT AT HER WHITE GRAND PIANO, gazing down at Central Park. She gave a small, pretty sigh, picked up her cell phone and called a number that rang two hundred miles away, in Washington DC, and caused Frank Costello to put down his cigar. He showed the screen to the other men sitting at the table and caused a generalized scramble.

"Priti, where the hell are you? The Feds are going crazy looking for you!"

She gave an elegant laugh and stood. "Frank, I am delighted to hear you too. Were you that worried you actually sent the FBI out looking for me?"

"No, Priti, I'm serious. They've been searching everywhere for you."

"The FBI? What on Earth do the FBI want with me?"

"Where *are* you, Priti?"

"I'm in my apartment in Manhattan! For goodness sake, Frank! Will you please tell me what is going on!"

"Hang on, I'm going to hand you over to Agent Hogan. He's a crap poker player, but he's a great cop."

Hogan took the phone. "Ms. Anand?"

"Miss, what is this all about, Agent Hogan?"

"I want you to listen very carefully to what I am going to tell you. Your life might be in danger."

"Is this some kind of joke? It is in very bad taste! Put Frank back on the phone immediately!"

"Shut up, Miss Anand. This is not a joke. This is Special Agent Sean Hogan, I am with Mr. Costello at a safe house and we have been searching for you and Mr. de Jong because we have reason to believe your lives are at risk. Do you understand me?"

She sank back onto her stool and glanced involuntarily at the door across the large, bright, empty room with its shiny black-and-white checkerboard floor.

"Yes," she said after a moment.

"Have you got security at your apartment?"

"I have a couple of bodyguards?"

"How long have you had them?"

"A couple of years. I trust them implicitly."

"Keep them with you at all times. Let no one into the apartment for any reason. I am going to send some agents from the New York Field Office. They will identify themselves to your bodyguards. Before you let them in you call the field office to confirm it's them. Understood?"

"Yes."

"Miss Anand, do you know where Mr. de Jong is?"

"Yes, we were at a spiritual retreat together in the Adirondacks. I think he is flying to San Francisco right now.

I'll give you his personal number and you can call him on his plane."

She gave him the number and heard him recite it to somebody else. Then he said to her, "Miss Anand, are your bodyguards with you now?"

"Not in this room, no."

"I want you to call them, and I want you to put the phone on loudspeaker, so I can talk to them. Understood?"

"Yes."

As she said it there was a tap at the door. It opened and a young man stepped in. Like all her waiting staff he had a burgundy blazer and black pants. She didn't recognize him, but she paid little attention to her staff. She noticed he was very small and pale, with very blue eyes and thin sandy hair. He held a silver tray with a martini on it.

"Go and get Akal," she told him, "and Randeep. Tell them to come to me immediately."

He bowed his head, crossed the floor and placed the martini on the piano. She frowned at him and said, "*Immediately!*"

He bowed again and left on quick, silent feet.

"They will be here in a moment, Agent Hogan. They are Sikhs, their English is very good. They are very loyal, faithful and quite lethal, I am told."

"Good."

There was another tap at the door and two men came in. They were both over six foot, built like barn doors, but athletic. They both had turbans, Akal had a thick black beard but Randeep was clean shaven.

Priti Anand placed her telephone on the piano. "I want

you both to listen very carefully to what Agent Hogan of the FBI has to say."

Hogan explained the situation again and they listened attentively.

"You stay with her at every moment. If she goes to the john you check the john first. When she goes to bed you check every entrance to the room. Understood?"

Akal said, "Understood."

Priti Anand reached for her martini. She raised it to her lips. Randeep stepped forward and placed his hand over the glass. She stared at him and he shook his head once. Then he took the glass from her fingers.

"I will make all your drinks and all your food from now on, *Meri a'Aurata*.[1]"

She nodded. He muttered something to Akal and left for the kitchen.

"Miss Anand?" It was the phone. "Are you still there?"

"Yes, Agent Hogan."

"The agents from our New York field office will be arriving soon. What we would like is for you to go with them so that they can take you to a secure location. Would you be willing to do that?"

She sighed and put her hand to her forehead. "Oh, my goodness, this is absurd. I have so much work to do! I *need* to be in New York!"

"Miss Anand..."

"Can't you just place a guard on my apartment until you catch this person? I am due to meet with Senator Costello, I am lunching with the mayor tomorrow..."

"Miss Anand!"

"Yes!"

"You are on a list."

"I *beg* your pardon?"

"You are on a hit list. You, Mr. de Jong and several other people. Mr. Costello is here with us because he is also on that list. Now, one of the people on that list has already been killed. Do you understand what I am telling you?"

"Johannes and Frank are on this list too?"

"Yes, and I am with Senator Costello right now. We will provide you with everything you need…"

"I'll have to bring my own IT."

"That's fine."

"My bodyguards and my PA, and at least a couple of staff."

"Just so long as they are people you have good reason to trust. Email me some form of ID, driver's license, social security number, something we can check up on. Meanwhile please get ready to ship out fast, and Miss Anand?

"Please be discreet. Make it look like you're going shopping, OK?"

"Excuse me?"

"No caravanserai of staff and trunks advertising that you're leaving, Miss Anand! You and your two bodyguards leave, no luggage. An hour later you send your PA and one member of staff with maximum two suitcases down to the parking garage and they leave."

"Two suitcases?"

"Miss Anand, get real! Right now, while we are speaking, somebody is making practical arrangements to kill you. Please, don't make it any easier for them."

"I understand."

A moment later Randeep returned with a sealed bottle of gin and a sealed bottle of martini. He showed the bottles to her. "Always from a sealed bottle," he said, "and only from a glass that Akal or I have washed."

She sighed and watched him mix the drink. "What about the ice?"

He smiled. "From plastic bags which I have prepared."

———

HELEN DROPPED two cubes of ice into her glass and asked Gallin, "Are you sure you won't have something?"

"Not on duty, thanks."

Helen carried her glass back to her desk across the deep blue carpet and sat. Behind her the Stars and Stripes declared her loyalty to the Federation, and the window showed an impressive view of Constitution Avenue, and the Capitol and its gardens beyond.

"I understand you are with the Mossad," she said, a little ambiguously.

"We often cooperate with American intelligence services," Gallin replied, equally ambiguously. Helen smiled.

"We seem to be fencing. That isn't what I want. You know I used to call Paul Uncle? He was like family. My grandparents were Jewish."

Gallin didn't smile. "You don't need Jewish credentials to talk to me, Senator Troy. Our purpose is to keep you and the other people on the list safe. What did you want to talk to me about?"

Senator Troy sighed. "Cut to the chase, huh? OK, I can

appreciate that. I called Paul on the day he died. On reflection it must have been shortly before he was killed."

"How did he sound?"

She seemed to shrug with her eyebrows. "He sounded normal. I knew Paul very well. I'd known him for years, since I was a kid. I think I would have been able to tell if there was something wrong. But on the other hand, I don't have to tell you, the Mossad are tough people who don't show their emotions."

"What did you talk about?"

The senator puffed out her cheeks. "I had asked him to talk to the ambassador."

"The Israeli Ambassador?"

"Yeah, Paul carried a lot of weight at the embassy. Because of his experience, his age and his intelligence, he was seen as a man of wisdom and a safe pair of hands. I knew that if Paul could persuade the ambassador that I was a good friend to Israel, and the ambassador let it be known that he favored me, that would give me a big boost among the Jewish community in the States." She paused to sip her drink. "I am sure you are aware, Captain Gallin, not only is the Jewish vote important for a future president, but having the support of the Jewish community."

Gallin gave a humorless smile. "We punch above our weight, and we move a lot of money for such a small country. So you tried to persuade him to get the ambassador on board, and he told you no."

"Pretty much, yeah. He didn't believe I would be a good friend to Israel, or the Jewish community in the States."

"Must've hurt."

"Yes."

"Was he right?"

Senator Troy gave a small, ironic laugh. "One shouldn't generalize, but you Israelis! It's like you're on fire. So intense. Paul was the same. Why waste time when you can go straight for the jugular?"

"We have very little space, Senator, and we never know how much time we have. Was he right?"

"We have to work with the Arabs, Captain. They are there and they own forty-three percent of the world's oil."

"If you'll forgive me saying so, Senator, 'work with' is an ambiguous phrase, and politicians are not people who are likely to commit themselves to anything down the line if they can possibly avoid it. To a man like Paul, Senator, he just didn't feel he could trust you. I'm sorry if that's unfeeling." The senator nodded at her desk and Gallin asked her, "Is this what you wanted to talk to me about? I am not sure what it is you want to tell me."

"Partly." She essayed a smile that didn't get very far. "I guess I wanted to talk to someone who knew Paul. I guess I feel a little guilty. We were like family, but I had been so involved with work lately, during his separation and divorce, I guess I feel I should have been there for him more. Now he's gone...and..." She paused, staring at Gallin, and took a deep breath. Gallin was surprised to see that the senator was crying. "I'm sorry. I'm not good with family issues. I am left with the memory that the last conversation I had with him, however innocently, I was trying to manipulate him for my own political ends. That was wrong."

Gallin waited. Eventually the senator started talking again.

"There was something else. I had a brief, ill-advised relationship with Jerry Feynman. Politics can be like that, Captain. It may be hard to understand from where you're sitting. But loyalty and friendship are hard to find in the political world. Everybody has an agenda, and power is the prize. I had long since lost my parents and my husband, and suddenly Jerry was there behaving like a friend. I guess I wanted to believe he was for real. Nobody else was."

Gallin said, "But Paul disapproved."

She nodded. "Very much. We had a couple of discussions and eventually a stand-up row. I demanded to know why he disliked Jerry so much and he told me. He told me Jerry was not only—in his words—a spineless cheat who would sell his mother to cannibals for the promise of political influence, he was also an out-and-out traitor who was in the pay of the Russians who had relied on him during the suitcase crisis, and were using him now to influence the president on international policy. In particular Ukraine and sanctions."

Gallin arched an eyebrow. "That surprised you?"

"I told him I didn't believe him and he told me he could provide me with proof."

"And did he?"

She shook her head. "No, but we made peace and now I am wondering if Paul didn't try to get proof, and paid the consequences."

"You think Jerry might have killed him?"

"No, Jerry would not kill anyone with his own hands. But he might have them killed. He certainly has the connections to have it done." She spread her hands. "I am sure you know your job, Captain. I have the greatest respect for the professionalism of the Mossad. But it may be worth talking to Paul's colleagues at the embassy and find out if he was investigating Paul."

———————

JUST DOWN THE ROAD, Jerry looked at his watch. "I have to go. People are going to start asking questions. Can we meet tonight?"

I leaned across the table to him and leered as I whispered, "You are being watched, Jerry, we have men on you twenty-four seven, and you know it's true. Try and do a runner, and I will have you shot. My department has zero accountability, Jerry. Just remember that. Where do you want to meet?"

He thought about it. "You know the RFK Stadium, by the Whitney Young Memorial Bridge?" I nodded. "There is a big parking lot there. It's always empty. There are some steel containers down by lot 8a. I'll meet you there tonight. Nine thirty."

I smiled and stood. "You know the place pretty well, huh? Enjoy your whisky."

He looked sullen, but I was done with him and I left.

Out on H Street my stomach was reminding me that it also mattered, in the wider scheme of things. I called Gallin and she told me, "I see you, I'm just arriving."

She pulled up on the pedestrian crossing. People honked at her, but it was like it wasn't happening in her particular version of the universe. I climbed in and we moved gently off toward Chinatown.

"How'd it go?"

"OK, I think. He wants to meet tonight in the parking

lot at the Robert F. Kennedy Stadium, by the Anacostia Park."

"He'll try to kill you?"

"What, a nice guy like me?"

"Let me tell you what Senator Helen Troy has to say about Jerry Feynman."

FOURTEEN

I sent her up Rhode Island Avenue via the Logan Circle, and we had a late lunch at the Red Hen on First Street. It is one of DC's rare little treasures, and just a ten-minute walk from my house. The walls are bare redbrick with wooden paneling to waist height. The tables are big and chunky and made of wood, with plenty of room for your elbows, and you get linen napkins to wipe your mouth with.

We grabbed a table by the window and a waitress in a black T-shirt came over and smiled. "Hello Mr. Mason," To Gallin she just said, "Hi, what can I get you?"

Gallin growled, "Get me a vodka martini, easy on the martini. We don't wanna drown it, right?"

The waitress showed a lot of teeth, whether through humor or fear wasn't clear. "Right," she said. I told her, "A beer," and she went away.

Gallin looked at me with intense brown eyes and said, "I want meat."

"Will I do?"

"Have you been braised over hot coals?"

I arched an eyebrow. "...yes?"

"Then you have a problem."

When the waitress came back with our drinks Gallin said, "I *need* a grilled Creekstone beef short rib. And all that other stuff?" She waved her fingers over the menu. "About the asparagus and the roast potatoes and the ramps and the mustard...? I need all that too."

The waitress did a cute little thing where she bounced on her knees and giggled. She looked at me and I told her I'd have the same. When she'd gone Gallin sipped her drink with restraint and said, "Jerry is the guy. I have to tell you I am glad because I have never liked him. He is not..." She leaned back in her chair, stretched out her legs and spread her hands expansively. "He is not 'crimes against humanity' bad. What can I tell you? He is not '*genocide*' bad. I can't say that, Mason, but he takes 'creep' bad to new heights. He has betrayed his country, sold influence to the Russians, probably murdered good, innocent people...," she pursed her lips and shook her head, "say the word and I will put a team on him. Oops! Fell backward onto a salad fork. Accidents will happen."

"Are you done, Gallin?"

"Don't know what to tell you, partner."

"Revving a little high, aren't we?"

"I liked Paul. I had a lot of respect for him. Ours is a tiny country, Mason. And it's lions like Paul who keep us safe. And this little prick killed him."

"You know that for sure?"

"Ninety percent."

"OK, take your foot off the gas, drink your vodka

martini and let's take it from the beginning, step by step. Then I'll tell you what he told me."

She was watching me quietly from under her brows. When I'd finished she said, "You know you're very attractive when you do that."

"What."

"You cut out the facetious crap, speak calmly and with authority. A woman could go for that. 'Cause you're kind of handsome, too." She moved her hand around her face. "Good bones. How come you never got married, Mason?"

"Gallin?"

"Yeah, OK. Foot off the gas. So, first thing she—Helen—was kind of keen for me to know that her grandparents were Jewish. Like she thought that would give her more credibility or something." She sat up and placed her elbows on the table, with the backs of her thumbs against her mouth. "She made a point of telling me she used to call Paul Uncle. He was like family. I had to keep prompting her to get to the point. Then she told me she had called Paul on the day he was killed at what must have been shortly before the time of the murder."

"No kidding." I reached for my cell. "Just hold on there a second, will you?" I dialed.

"Hey, Mason. Ted here. What can I do for you?"

"You check on those calls I asked you to prioritize?"

"Yeah. There is only one in the time frame you were interested in. It's listed in his address book as Minnie."

"Give me the number, will you?"

I jotted it down and he added, "He also mentions a Minnie in a notebook where he seems to have noted down phrases, bits of poetry, odd stuff."

"Yeah?" I thought a moment. "OK, thanks Ted."

I dialed. It rang three times and a cautious voice said, "Yes?"

"Senator Troy?"

"Yes. Mr. Mason? How did you..."

"Just checking the number, Senator. Nothing to worry about."

I hung up and stared at Gallin's face for a moment. "So she is Minnie—"

"Helena Mila Talman. Minnie. Troy by marriage. Can I go on now?"

I made an affirmative "Hmmm..." and nodded.

"So I asked her how he'd seemed when she called. She said he seemed OK. I asked her what they talked about. She said she'd called because she'd been asking him to talk to the Israeli ambassador and tell him Helen was a good friend of Israel. That he should spread the word among the Jewish community to back her for nomination."

"But he wouldn't play ball."

"You going to tell me or am I going to tell you?"

"Tell me."

"He wouldn't play ball because he knew she wanted to get in bed with the Arabs. He didn't believe, if she did that, that she could be a good friend to Israel, or the Jewish community in the States. That must have hurt. She really liked this guy. Her parents were dead and so was her husband. He was about the only person she had she could trust."

I made a noncommittal noise and she went on. "Anyhow, so I am beginning to get antsy and I ask her why she's asked me to go over there. So she tells me there was something else."

"Jerry."

"Jerry. Apparently she had a brief affair with him."

I made a face like I'd bitten into a lemon and said, "*Why?* Why do women *do* that?"

"I don't know, Mason. I think the hormones get the better of them, they do something stupid and then regret it in the morning, when it's too late. Anyhow, she said he was nice to her, the whole big bad Washington DC rat race was getting to her, she was lonely yadda yadda yadda, so she thought she'd snuggle up with the dirtiest rat in the race.

"Not surprisingly, Paul disapproved. Called him a spineless cheat who would sell his mother to cannibals in exchange for political influence. He also claimed Jerry was an out and out traitor who was in the pay of the Russians. He said the Russians had relied on him during the suitcase crisis, and were using him now to influence the president to ease up on sanctions."

"Could he back any of that up?"

"That's what she asked him, and he said he would give her proof. Shortly after that, *before* he was able to provide proof, he was killed."

"After he called Jerry."

"I asked her if she thought Jerry had killed him. She said, and I quote verbatim: 'No, Jerry would not kill anyone with his own hands. But he might have them killed. He certainly has the connections to have it done.' Then she suggested I talk to Paul's colleagues at the embassy, to find out if he was investigating Jerry."

I frowned. "Surely they would have come forward."

"Meh." She kind of winced. "Intelligence agencies don't like sharing. You know that. If they know ODIN is involved, maybe they'd hold back. Do they need ODIN? Maybe not. Will they want to handle it their own way? Maybe. You know you do the same thing."

"OK, I hear you. So pull some strings. I have a meeting with Jerry this evening, as I told you. He held up his hands, said 'You got me fair and square,' and this evening, under the pretext of confessing all, he is going to try and kill me."

"I'll be there to stop him."

"You bet your cute little rump you will."

"May I shoot him, please?"

"Not unless it's necessary, Gallin. We need to debrief this guy. We have a big problem with Russian infiltration, and we seriously need to deal with that."

She gave a small shrug. "OK."

We had ice cream instead of whiskey and I paid the bill. As the waitress went away Gallin said, "Nice place. We should come again. Next one's on me, and we round off with margaritas instead of ice cream. Your house is staggering distance, right?"

"Yeah, c'mon, I'll show you. We'll have coffee and talk about tonight."

We spent the rest of the afternoon talking things over from every angle and drinking coffee. We even drew a few diagrams of the parking lot in question, which lay beside the Anacostia River.

At seven or thereabouts we took a drive and collected an unremarkable Toyota from the ODIN fleet of unremarkable cars and she made her way, by winding routes, to the RFK Stadium. There she parked in Zone 8 near some big steel containers, went to reconnoiter the area and vanished from sight. I, meanwhile, went home, had a shower and a shave, armed myself with a Sig Sauer P226 in a pancake in the small of my back, and at shortly before nine I climbed into my Roadster and headed for the stadium.

I got there at fifteen minutes past. Dusk had already closed in and night was settling on the city as I came in along Independence Avenue. I had the monolith of the RFK Stadium looming on my left, and the darkness of Anacostia Park and the river on my right, beyond the dead glow of the tall, spindly lamps in the empty acres of the parking lot.

I took the exit and rolled into the parking lot. It stretched out for acres to left and right, and ahead of me down toward Kingman Lake and the river. All I could see was empty concrete lots in the dead, yellow glow of the lamps. But over to my right, about two hundred yards away, I could see the silver glint of a giant metal container dumped by the side of the lots. I spun the wheel and crossed the lot.

I came to a towering lamppost with two lights spread out like a bat's wings. It bore a sign that told me this was lot eight, where Jerry had said to meet him. There was a scattering of cars with black windows like blind, dead eyes. Among them I spotted Gallin's unremarkable Toyota, and felt glad she was there. I couldn't see her, but I knew she was watching me right then. I parked beside the lamppost and killed my headlamps. Then fixed my eyes on the mirror.

Nothing happened for ten minutes or maybe a little more. Then I saw a set of headlamps. They came in off the highway and didn't slow, then turned toward where I was parked and crossed the lot. As they got closer I saw it was a dark SUV. It pulled in a few spaces away and killed the lights.

After a moment Jerry got out, poked a cigarette in his mouth and lit it, letting the glow from his disposable lighter illuminate his face for a few seconds.

I climbed out and crossed the ten yards between us, aware of the weight of my P226 on my lower back. "Good evening, Jerry. Are we going to talk out here? Have you got a scope on me right now?"

He took a long drag and held the smoke before letting it out in a long stream. The habit of a long-term marijuana smoker. "What makes you think I want you dead, Mason?"

I laughed. "The fact that I am getting ready to nail you for treason, spying for the Russians and murdering the security attaché at the Israeli Embassy seem like a few damn good reasons, Jerry."

"Well," he shrugged, "that shows what you know. Would it surprise you if I told you that from where I am sitting, you're doing me a big favor?"

"Nothing you say would ever surprise me, Jerry. I'd think it was bullshit, but it wouldn't surprise me."

He sighed and flicked ash, looking down at his shoes.

"I've got kids, Mason. Did you know that?"

"Yeah, I've read your file, Jerry. You have two girls, seven and ten. Is this where you tell me the Russians blackmailed you by threatening your kids?"

He shook his head. "I don't blame you for being skeptical. It was a few years back, when people were starting to notice me and the reports I was writing, and I was getting invited to the West Wing for debriefing. Pretty soon the president was calling me on my personal phone to discuss issues. You're cynical, but I am pretty good at what I do."

"Yeah, life's unfair like that. Cut to the chase."

"So one day, four or five years ago, this British guy calls me and says he wants to talk to me. I was about to tell him to go to hell and he mentions my kids. Anyway, long story short, I agree to meet him. He says his name is Sebastian, it's obviously a fake name, he's tall, slim, very blond, pale blue eyes. He has what the Brits call a cut-glass accent. He talks like Hugh Grant. You get the idea."

"I get the idea, Jerry."

"So he tells me he represents a group of lobbyists who would like to pay me a lot of money, and all I have to do is recommend certain ideas and policies to the president."

"Naturally you were scandalized and told them to go to hell."

"I wasn't scandalized, Mason. I've been in the game too long for that. But I did tell him to go to hell because believe it or not I am a patriot."

"Sure, so you told him to go to hell. Then what?"

"He said he was very sorry to hear that, and that he would have to offer the money to my wife, instead. I asked him what the hell he was talking about, and he told me he understood she had very valuable information to sell about me, about how I abused my daughters and was violent to her. I told him it would never stick and he told me 'Shit always sticks.'"

He dropped his cigarette butt on the ground and crushed it with his toe.

"So I should have resigned, trusted my wife, gone to the Feds. But right then all I could see was that whatever I did, I would lose my position next to the president, which I had busted my balls for, for so long. I told myself, 'What harm can it do? I'll only push policies that benefit the USA. And I'd do that anyway, right? And I could use a couple of hundred grand a year. Who couldn't?" He reached in his pocket for a pack of Camels and shook one free. It was a fresh pack. He showed it to me. "I'd quit. Now I figure, what the hell have I got to lose?"

He lit it, inhaled deeply through his teeth and spoke as he released the smoke.

"It was stupid, naïve, deluded. Whatever you like. For four years I took the money and was barely aware of their presence. Then the suitcases came along and they started to turn the screws: Advise the president that it's a hoax, advise the president to play it down, protect the stock market... It was credible advice. It was *bad* advice, but it was credible. They were legitimate concerns, but any fool could see that we had to be out there hunting that damned nuke. You saw that, and so did the Israelis."

"Paul approached you?"

"Yeah, he called the president. They were friends. He said he wanted to talk to me discreetly in his office at the embassy. I didn't want to go but I had no choice. Paul knew exactly what was going on. He questioned me for almost an hour. I later discovered he recorded every word, bugged my car and also bugged my phone. He put my house under surveillance, used laser technology that apparently doesn't even exist yet to eavesdrop on my conversations and tapped my phone. He built a file on me the size of the Old Testament."

"At first he just wanted to make sure you weren't a threat to Israel. But then he discovered you were having an affair with Helen Troy."

He went quiet and stared at me for a long moment. "Word gets around, huh?"

"In DC? Are you kidding me? What were you doing, grooming the next potential president?"

"As it happens, I like her. She is one of the few honest people in this town."

"Two beautiful souls brought together in the heart of the rat race. You should sell it to Hollywood. So what happened next? He told you to back off, right?"

"He did more than that. He told me he wanted half a million bucks and he wanted me to break it off with Helen."

I laughed. "Are you serious? Half a million bucks?"

"I told Helen he'd warned me off. She said she'd talk to him. But he called me, the day he was killed, and said the price had risen to a million bucks and would keep rising daily until I paid. He was one tough son of a bitch."

"So what happened? You sent someone to kill him?"

He looked at me like I was a mental retard. "Let me ask you something, genius. If I was going to have him killed, would I pay him a million bucks?"

"You paid him?"

"Of course I paid him! If I didn't pay him I was going to spend the rest of my goddamn life in prison. You can check my bank records."

"So you paid him and then killed him. That's a pretty good defense."

"No, a good defense is to pay him two hundred or two hundred and fifty grand and then kill him. A million bucks is crazy."

He had a point.

"What about Helen?"

"Since you showed up she's busy all the time, washing her hair. She doesn't want to know me anymore. So what happens now? I've collaborated, I've helped you. You come against me and you will embarrass the president. That will not be appreciated."

"Well, that's a big shame, Jerry. Because now you go to prison for the rest of your miserable life, Jerry."

"What?" He shook his head and even laughed. "No, you don't understand. I have friends who can bury you, pal. We do a deal. I give you all this and you give me immunity."

"All what? That Colonel Paul Hirschfield was doing the FBI's job for them? Get real, Jerry! Come on, turn around!"

"Goddammit, Mason! I thought we had an understanding!"

"You thought wrong—again! Turn around!"

My only excuse is that I was expecting a gun, not a fist like a hunk of concrete. I reached for the Sig behind my back, and while I was doing that he smashed that fist right into the side of my head. The world went black and I went down.

FIFTEEN

I MUST HAVE BEEN OUT FOR ONLY A SECOND. Because I was suddenly aware of him kneeling on me and trying to reach for my weapon—a position which brought his right kidney within striking difference of my left hand. It wasn't an easy blow but I gave it all I had, and followed up by smashing the heel of my right hand into his nose. Because of my position, on my back and with a broken brain, it didn't do much more than annoy him, which led him to sit astride me, take a handful of his shirt in his left hand and pull his right fist back for a killer punch to the jaw.

There is a surprisingly easy way out of that kind of situation, but you have to be quick, and all your movements have to be simultaneous and very, very aggressive.

I grabbed his left wrist in my left hand, and hammered the heel of my right hand into his elbow like my life depended on it, three times. That hurt him a lot and made him pull his arm away.

That's when you go into phase two.

I enjoy watching MMA and cage fights, but I often wonder at the advanced yoga contortions guys go into sometimes to dislodge an opponent who is sitting astride them. In a no-holds-barred street fight that is not necessary. Though again you have to be fast.

You grab a fistful of their shirt with your left hand, pull yourself up and smash your fist into their balls—two or three times.

He made a noise like air being sucked through a closed door and fell on his side clutching at what was left of his family jewels. Maybe he was thinking of all the little Jerries he was never going to make. I got slowly and painfully to my feet and looked around for Gallin. I saw her approaching at a relaxed walk from the direction of the container.

"Thank God you were here," I said with just a twist of bitterness.

She shook her head. "I am going to have to take you in hand, dude, and teach you to fight. You should never have let him get on top of you that way."

"Yeah, yeah. Did you get all that?"

"Every word. Team's on its way to take him in for interrogation and secure the SUV." She gently punched my shoulder, like she was about to say something nice. "Seriously, though, dude. Too much whiskey and champagne, too many oysters, you should have seen that punch coming. You want me to teach you a few moves, huh? Bit of JKD, bit of Krav Maga?"

"Keep it up and you sleep on the couch tonight."

She surprised me by gasping, then said, "Oh! Oh!" a few times and finally shut up. By that time two large dark vans had appeared on the highway and were pulling into the parking lot. They were about as inconspicuous as a naked Schwarzenegger walking into a Hell's Angel club and saying, "Gimme your cloze." They were extracting one guy and could have done it in a Honda Civic. But maybe in DC that would have drawn too much attention.

They pulled up beside us and four guys in dark suits with shades and wires in their ears climbed out. For a moment it was like being on the fringes of a schizophrenics' convention, with everyone looking around at invisible objects and talking to themselves. Finally a big black guy looked left, right and above my head and said, "Are you Mason?"

"Are you talking to me?"

He said, "Yes," and before I could answer, "Perimeter clear. Confirm bundle. Extraction active in T-minus fifty-nine and counting."

"What."

"Are you Mason?"

"Yes!"

"I need you to confirm my ID," he said to the space beside my head, and showed me his ODIN-Pentagon card. I looked at it. "Will you authorize extraction of the bundle to HQ? Check."

"What?"

He sighed and slipped his shades down his nose to look at me. "Mr. Mason, the chief sent me to collect that." He pointed to Jerry, who was being lifted to his feet by the other three Men in Black. "Can I take him?"

"Yes."

"Thank you."

Halfway to the van he stopped and turned back. "I have

like five different voices in my head at the same time some-times. All talkin' in code."

"That's not good."

He climbed in the van and they all drove away, except that one of them took Gallin's unremarkable Toyota. I looked at her. "Is it me or was that kind of surreal?"

"You."

"Oh."

"So we need to go and think about this, Mason." I nodded. "I would suggest burgers and beer, somewhere quiet, and we put all the bits together on a paper napkin."

"Yeah." I nodded, still feeling woozy and with a big pain in my head.

"You've got bruises on your face," she said, narrowing her eyes at me. "We could go to the Ugly Mug on 8th Street, but they might think you're part of the staff." She started to giggle. "We'd better go to the Hawk 'n' Dove on Pennsyl-vania Avenue."

I sighed and made for my Mk4 Roadster. "You are defi-nitely sleeping on the sofa tonight."

We went to the Hawk 'n' Dove by way of the Capitol Hill Pharmacy, where I bought a large number of painkillers, while wondering if everything in DC had some kind of political theme in the name. I mentioned it to Gallin as we sat at a table outside the pub and ordered a couple of beers and a couple of hamburgers with all the trimmings.

"Yup," she said. "It's like the Catholics. In Catholic countries you get things like the Sacred Blood of Jesus Laun-dromat, or the Sacred Heart of Mary Bakery, Virgin of the Eternal Sorrows Drugstore. In DC politics is like a religion, so you get the same thing, Off the Record, Hawk 'n' Dove, Capitol Pharmacy. How's your face?"

"How's your face?"

"Fine, how's yours?"

She started to laugh and after I'd washed down a couple of painkillers with a rich IPA I started to laugh too.

When we were about halfway through our burgers Nero called.

"Sir," I said without enthusiasm, "I was just toying with the idea of maybe sleeping this week."

There was a moment's silence. Then, "Are you telling me this for any particular reason?"

"No, sir."

"Do you know South Hangman Tree Road?"

"That's..." I hesitated a moment. "In the forest?"

"Precisely. Where Hangman intersects with MCB1, go south for half a mile and you will find a break in the trees that leads into a small clearing. There you will find a large house largely hidden by the canopy."

"OK—"

"This is where we have kept Costello until now. De Jong and Priti Anand have agreed to put themselves under our protection at this site. Feynman has been brought to a facility nearby for interrogation. I should be grateful if you and Captain Gallin would join us here, if that does not interfere too much with your sleeping arrangements."

"Yes, of course, sir. What about Senator Troy?"

"She has declined. She feels the protection she has at home is sufficient." There was a fleeting hint of humanity in his voice when he added, "I would suggest ten AM tomorrow."

"Thank you, sir."

I hung up and smiled at Gallin. "We get to rest till tomorrow morning."

The burgers arrived and we ordered more beer and sat in exhausted, companionable silence, watching the evening strollers drift by.

"It's the order," I said after a while.

She glanced at me and bit into her burger. "Mumph?"

"Why start with Paul Hirschfield? Then go all the way to Los Angeles to eliminate James Reed, when he had Helen Troy just ten or fifteen miles away? And she was at the top of the list and underscored twice. If you were working through a hit list, wouldn't you go for the underscored person at the top of the list first?"

"I always have done," she said without smiling.

"Helen and Paul first, then Costello who was also in DC at the time, and he must have known that, and *then* Reed on the other side of the country."

"So, the list is not in order of priority. The names were jotted down, and the order of priority was given orally, while they were discussing it."

"In that case, why is Helen underscored?"

She sighed, wiped her fingers and picked up her beer.

"Because this is a punishment list. And whoever made this list knew that Paul and Senator Troy were close, and killing one would hurt the other." She chewed her lip a moment, eyeing me. "Paul was like a father figure to her, right?"

"She called him uncle."

"She's been straying a little from the fold. Screwing

around with Jerry Feynman, cozying up with people who were not friends of Israel, so he calls her to order…"

"Wait." I raised my hand. "Jerry is in bed with the Russians…"

"Yes." She snapped her fingers. "And he has promised them he can get Troy to work for them. But when the time comes to deliver, Paul is too strong an influence on her and she tells Jerry to take a hike. So they kill Paul, and *that* is why her name is underscored, because she is the target in another sense."

"What do you mean, a target in another sense?"

"They kill Paul to make her see they mean business. If she still doesn't go over and work for them, *then* they kill her, or someone in her family."

"Huh… So they're using Jerry to recruit."

"Which would mean that the person behind the list is Jerry's handler."

"Why her?" I asked. "Why not Costello or Reed?"

"Because," she said, and gazed out at the slow, stop-and-start flow of the traffic. "*Because* it is a punishment list. Everyone on the list started out dancing to the Russian tune, supporting greater cooperation with Russia; and they were vocal about the suitcase bombs being a scam. But then, when the bomb was actually found, they changed their tune. So they all have to be punished."

I nodded slowly, letting my mind flow with the idea. "Except Costello, who was an out-and-out opponent from the start, and they don't want him in the White House, and Helena Troy, whom they want to secure as their woman in Congress and, hopefully, in the White House."

"Neat."

I showed her a bunched-up face that said I didn't think it was that neat. "So the second page of the list?"

"What about it?"

"None of the people on that list is a politician, or involved in politics. All three are government agents." She grunted. I went on. "That is a real punishment list. You bin bad, you gonna die."

"That's not funny. You're on that list." She shrugged. "It is just an extension of the original list, Mason. Don't complicate things."

I nodded. "I guess you're right. Come on, let's go get some sleep. I want to be wide awake when I talk to Priti Anand and de Jong tomorrow. I also want to have another go at Jerry Feynman."

She drove because my head still hurt. We took 2nd Street up as far as M Street and cut across under the railway bridge, where people live in tents and dumpsters in the capital city of the richest nation on Earth. Gallin looked at them without expression and muttered, "I guess this is the dark side of opportunity."

"Everyone has a right to be a loser."

She looked at me to see if I was being ironic. I wasn't sure myself.

"Not every problem has a social solution," she said.

"Yeah, but I suspect people living in tents under a railway bridge is a problem that does have a social solution."

"Maybe."

She said it in that voice that tells you the person is only agreeing because they don't want to argue. I studied her face a moment.

"You're pretty hard, huh, Gallin?"

"Very. We live in hell, Mason. We are born into hell. You fight or you go under. And anyone who tries to pull you out, gets pulled under too. All you can do is help people to help themselves. But the bottom line? You have to do it yourself."

"That's a pretty bleak view."

"It's not bleak, it's not rosy." She pointed through the windshield at the intersection with First Street. "That is the intersection with First Street NE. I can pretend it's the intersection with Fifth Street as long as I like, but it won't change the fact. It is what it is. We live in a world where we have to eat each other in order to survive. That's the measure of the situation."

We eventually turned right onto First Street NW and from there it was five minutes, past the Red Hen, to Adam Street and my home. It was gone eleven by the time we got there. The bleep of the car echoed down the silent street as I climbed the stairs, and I heard Gallin's feet climbing behind me. I unlocked the door and stood back for her to go inside. She flipped on the light and looked around, then gave me an odd, schoolgirl smile.

"It's nice."

"You want a nightcap?"

She grinned. "No, I want to go to bed."

On the way up the stairs she asked me, "You got a toothbrush I can borrow?"

"Sure. I have half a dozen unopened."

She laughed quietly. "You dawg."

I ignored her and showed her her room. She gave me that odd look again and asked, "This is where I sleep?"

I nodded and she followed me back to my room, asking, "So what time do you get up? Six, seven?"

"About that."

I closed the bathroom door, stripped, brushed my teeth, pulled on my pajamas and prepared for bed. My head was aching and my eyes were closing, I was so tired. I opened the bathroom door, switched off the light and, in the glow from the landing, I saw Gallin, stretched out on the bed in her jeans and her blouse, asleep and gently snoring.

I sighed. Then I smiled. I removed her boots, went to the wardrobe and pulled out a blanket. I threw it gently over her, taking care not to wake her, and got into bed beside her. We were separated by the duvet which was over me and under her, and there was also the barrier of her clothes. So I was not quite so intensely aware of her femininity. At least, that's what I told myself just before I closed my eyes. But as I drifted off into sleep I felt a movement beside me and a moment later she had nuzzled the top of her head into my armpit and slung her leg over both of mine. If it had been a guy, I would have pushed him off. But it was just Gallin. I smiled. It was Gallin.

A tenth of a second later I was deeply asleep.

SIXTEEN

I WAS AWOKEN BY THE SMELL OF COFFEE, BACON and eggs. I looked at the bedcovers and they were a tangled mess. The window showed a gray glimmer of dawn and my watch said it was just after six. I swung out of bed, experimented with my head and vision and decided I felt OK. So I had a shower and went down for breakfast.

She had four crusty rolls fresh out of the oven in a basket wrapped in a linen napkin, a plate full of bacon, four eggs and a pot of coffee. She had also found my favorite pot of English marmalade.

"How'd you sleep?" she asked with no particular inflexion.

"Good, well, I think. I see you found everything."

"Yeah," she said, pulling out a chair and sitting. "I thought you needed building up."

"Oh." I sat.

She waved her fork at me like a remonstrating finger. "I think we have a problem."

"Oh?"

"We know nothing about this killer, except that he's small, right?"

"Yes."

But he knew where Paul was, at home, when he should have been at his office. And he went directly to LA to kill Reed, and George Malkin, and obviously knew where they were."

"Because they were involved in organizing it."

"My point exactly. This is not one small man working on his own. He is backed by a team who ensure he knows exactly where his next victim is, at the moment he chooses to strike."

I frowned with my coffee halfway to my face. "Yeah, that's true, but we sort of took that for granted."

"Well sometimes it pays to think through the things you take for granted, buster. Because now we are gathering all his intended victims into one place…"

"All except one."

"The one whose name was underscored."

I went to stand. "I have been very stupid. We need to get to her house right now."

I was reaching for my phone and she was rolling her eyes.

"Relax, will you. I already called they guy who's heading up her security team."

"The ODIN team? How'd you get his number?"

"I called Nero too."

"You've been busy."

"Yeah, I also made breakfast. So I spoke to Nero and told him I didn't like the idea of all the intended victims gathered in one place. He said that place was impregnable. I told him nowhere was impregnable and he told me the decision was not up for discussion. So I told him how about the fact that the person who was underscored as the most important target was the one person not present at his impregnable fortress? He wasn't amused by that."

"I imagine he wasn't."

"I told him he needed to send another team and put the local PD on red alert. He said he would also alert the Secret Service. I told him we would arrive later than planned because we would go and See Helen first. So sit down and finish your breakfast."

"Why didn't we see all this last night, Gallin?"

Because we were tired, we had been too long without sleep and you had been hit in the head with a brick. Now, what are we going to do about Senator Troy?"

"We go get her. If we have to we put her in a sack, and we take her to Nero's safe house."

"How safe is it? This team sounds like it is skilled."

I shrugged. "It has to be one of the areas of highest security in the USA. It's Quantico. You've got the Feds, the Marines, the FBI labs, the FBI Academy, DEA Academy, the Marine Corps Embassy Security Group..."

"Yeah, OK, so that's a lot of security, but none of it is directed toward locating a small rat of a guy that nobody would notice unless you were looking for him."

"So we need her as a bait."

She grunted. "Now you're talking my language. Let's discuss it in the car. Eat your bacon."

I did as I was told and twenty minutes later we were bowling along the George Washington Memorial Parkway at a hundred plus miles per hour. At Scott's Run we came off onto the Georgetown Pike and Gallin said, "We can't force her, and something tells me she will not allow herself to be persuaded. Politicians see this kind of situation as good publicity. While everyone else was hiding, she was doing her duty. You know the kind of thing."

"Yeah, I know."

"They don't usually think about how many agents they might get killed while doing their duty."

"No, that's not the kind of thing they tend to think about. But what you're thinking about is if she insists on staying home and going to the office, we could watch her and move in if the killer shows. It is very risky."

"What else have we got?"

I glanced at her, with the trees and the beautiful old houses speeding past behind her.

"I don't know until we start grilling our witnesses."

She shook her head. "We don't have a lot of time to be doing things by the book."

I turned away and stared at the beautiful Virginia land-scapes around us. They had an air of venerable stability about them.

"We are losing our grip on this thing," I said, half-thinking aloud, then turned back to face Gallin. She pushed her glasses up on her head and long strands of hair were whipping around her face. "It's getting away from us. I thought we had something with Jerry. But my gut is telling me that was just a red herring."

"I don't agree, Mason. I think we have an execution list that was sent down by an official in Moscow. It probably has total plausible deniability, but what we have is a team with instructions from Moscow, to punish and eliminate those who promised support and failed to give it during and after the suitcase bombings."

I thought about it. "You're right."

"Sorry? What? Come again?"

"You're right, Gallin. You're right. What we need to do is set up a trap that not even Nero knows about. Just you and me."

She grinned. "I like it."

"Senator Troy is our tethered goat, you are absolutely right. She has made a choice of her own free will. It's up to us to make the most of that decision."

"How?" She frowned. "What's that?"

I looked ahead where she was pointing. Just beyond the intersection where we would turn east to go to her house, there was a clearing on the right where several cars were parked. About half of them were the kind of SUVs used by law enforcement and security services.

I said, "Roll up, let's have a look."

We moved past the intersection and pulled in beside a dark blue Audi.

We were in the parking lot of an old church. It was small, well kept and looked like it might be three or four hundred years old. There were rose beds out front flanking three stone steps, and in back it had oaks and chestnuts. It even had a holy tree trained over the door, to keep the witches out.

There was a crowd of people out front too, standing with the vicar and a woman I recognized as Helen Troy. She had four big goons in suits and shades standing around her and one giant standing next to her. He wasn't wearing shades and you could see his steady gaze taking in everything as he looked over the small crowd, every vehicle beyond the crowd, every house and every road. In fact, right then, as I climbed out of the car, he was staring straight at me.

Gallin slammed her door and came and stood next to me. "Big guy's her bodyguard, right?"

"I'd say so. First time I went to her house I think I saw him cleaning the car."

"He's in love with her."

I smiled at her. "Yeah?" I looked back at the giant by her side. "I think I believe you. Let's go see what's going on."

As we approached it became clear Senator Troy was giving an improvised soapbox speech, and it also became clear that a couple of the guys in the crowd were local press. One of them was taking pictures and a couple of the others were recording and making notes.

"...because we are more than a nation. We are a federation of peoples united by a series of ideals which were enshrined for us by our founding fathers in our Constitution. The ideals of liberty, freedom from oppression and the innate rights of Man have been the mainstay of our nation throughout the centuries and have fueled our spirits in times of war and adversity. So, to answer your question..." There was a burst of polite laughter. "Am I going to go into hiding because my name is on a list belonging to a rumored hit man? No. I am not. Let him come here to my constituency, and my constituents and I will show him how Americans deal with people who try to interfere with our internal affairs."

I glanced at Gallin. She sighed. "Somebody has leaked the list."

"But only to the local press."

"By tonight it will be all over the country."

She gave her ironic smile a bitter twist. "Yeah, but as it's not a major leak, nobody will suspect her."

Senator Troy's eyes caught mine. She didn't look friendly.

"Mr. Mason. You don't plan to leave me in peace, do you?"

"You should not be discussing this with the press, Senator."

"We have a free press in this country, you are aware of that?"

"Yeah, last time I checked we still had one, in spite of the best efforts of the White House. But this is a confidential matter that affects national security." I turned to the boys from the local press. "Tell your editors my office will be in touch—that's the Pentagon—you don't publish and you don't sell the story if you want a job by Monday. Scram."

I nodded to the vicar who had startled round eyes, took Troy's elbow and started guiding her toward her Jaguar as I spoke to her half-dozen security guards plus her chauffer.

"Gather round, boys. Hide the target."

"Mr. Mason, this is really very tiresome. Your boss was on the phone to me yesterday and again last night. And now he has sent you two to try and strong-arm me..."

"Shut up, Senator." I said it very mildly and pleasantly, as one might say, "Have another tuna and cucumber sandwich."

She stopped dead in her tracks and stared at me. Before she could say, "I *beg* your pardon!" as I knew she was planning to, I said, "We have to pull some of the boys off you. Right now you have more Secret Service men protecting you than the president. That's why we were keen to take you to our secure location."

"So it's blackmail! Either do what the department says or face the consequences!"

"Not really. We just haven't got the budget to provide every narcissistic senator who wants to put on a show of bravery for the TV cameras double the bodyguards the president gets, while they prance around putting their bodyguards' lives at risk."

"Boy, you're a real charmer." She started walking again.

"Again, not really. I only appear to be. I am actually a very unpleasant person." I smiled sweetly. "Ask Jerry. Now, Senator, I have important information for you. Are you prepared to be quiet while I brief you?"

We had reached her Jaguar and she turned to face me.

"If you have information for me, kindly brief me now."

I looked around at the bodyguards. "Here? Now? What kind of clearance have you boys got?" Nobody said anything. I added, "Give us some space, will you?"

The Secret Service boys moved off but her driver stayed put by her side, eyeballing me. She smiled at me like she'd scored a point. "You said keep him by you at all times, remember? That's what I told him to do and that's what he does. According to your instructions."

I frowned at her. "Why do you see me as the enemy, Senator? I am working my ass off to keep you safe, and you treat me like I am some kind of an opponent."

She smiled. "Does that hurt your ego, Mr. Mason?"

I gave my head a small twitch. "Not really, it just makes me wonder why. We are going to leave two Secret Service agents outside your house. And two of our men inside. Plus your driver," I looked at him a moment, "what's your name?"

He had a voice like distant thunder. "Isileli Manu."

I nodded. "You were washing the car the other day, right?"

It was like talking to a statue. "Maybe."

"Mason?" I looked back at her. "What is this? You're asking my driver if he was washing my car?"

I nodded. "Yeah, I ask a lot of questions. It's a habit. Till we sort this out Captain Gallin and I will be sitting outside your house at night. If you go anywhere, we'll follow you. We'd appreciate it if you touched base from time to time and let us know how you are and what you're doing."

She drew breath. Gallin cut her short. "We don't plan to encroach on your Second Amendment rights, Senator. I happen to be a fan of the Second Amendment. We just want to keep you safe."

"You done? Is the show over? Right. I now plan to go home, lock myself in my study with Isileli a shout away if I need him. I will work till about ten, with a short break for dinner. Then I will go to bed, feeling safer knowing that Isileli is down the hall, and you two are just outside. Good day."

Isileli opened the rear door of the Jag for her and she made to climb in.

"You know everybody else on the list will be at the secure location," I said. She stopped with one foot inside the car. She looked at me and I went on. "Of all the people listed who are not already dead, you are the only one who will not be foregathered there."

"What's your point?"

"My point is that it makes you a prime target."

She pushed her shades up on her head and squinted at me in the morning sun.

"From what you tell me, I was already a prime target."

I nodded a few times and was about to speak when Gallin cut in.

"I'm not sure how smart you are to take that attitude, Senator. Your personal assistant and one of your closest friends are already dead. Logic dictates that tonight or tomorrow he'll come for you."

"I don't really care how smart you think I am, Captain, and I am well aware of my friends and my colleagues who have been killed. If this bastard comes for me, I plan to be where he can find me. Is there anything else?"

"Yeah," I said, and she looked slightly surprised. "You didn't answer my earlier question. Why the attitude? Why the hostility? Is this how you thank the men and women who protect you and your country?"

I saw her eyes flick to the Secret Service boys, and knew she was thinking about the patriotic vet vote. She sighed and surprised me by looking embarrassed.

"You are absolutely right, Mr. Mason, and I owe you an apology. This situation has caused a lot of stress and anxiety, and I guess I have taken it out on you, quite unfairly. Please forgive me."

"No apology needed, Senator. I was just curious."

She climbed in the back of the Jag, pulled out of the lot and headed off with one dark SUV in front of her and two behind.

Two of those SUVs would right about now be receiving

orders to head back to DC. What would happen to Senator Helen Troy then? I wondered.

My cell rang and I answered without looking at the screen.

"Yeah, Mason."

The voice that answered was extremely cultured and English. "Hello, Mason. How are you?"

I scowled rather unfairly at Gallin, who looked curious. "Who is this?"

"I'm sorry. Did I catch you at a bad time? It's Peter, Peter Belov."

SEVENTEEN

"You sound pretty good for a dead guy."

I climbed in the car and gestured Gallin to lean close. If I put him on speaker he'd notice, and I didn't want him to know there was someone else listening.

There was a quiet laugh. "Death comes in many forms, Mason. Some are more agreeable than others. Are you alone?"

"Yes, you caught me in my car."

"Mm-hmm. Are you busy? Have you time to speak for a moment?"

"I always have time for you, Peter."

"That's very flattering. I have some information for you."

"OK."

"You may have noticed that the USA has been under a sustained attack from Russia in the last couple of months."

"I had noticed that, yes."

"There is a team, in the Kremlin, who are driving this

attack. It flows originally from the president, but it is channeled through, and nurtured by, a small team led by a woman who has a deep and abiding hatred for the United States."

"A woman? What's her name?"

"No, not over the telephone, old chap. Let's meet. I am in the States right now. Can you make it this evening?"

"Where and when?"

"You know Bethesda?"

"Of course."

"Seven Locks Road, on the corner with Rosehill Drive. You'll see a house there with a gabled roof and a double garage to the side of the house. Come alone, Mason. I am running a huge risk as it is. It would be a shame to stupidly screw things up."

"You've got it. What time?"

"Say nine thirty o'clock? I'll give you the information and I'd like to ask some favors from you. Deal?"

"Sure, we can talk. No problem."

"Good, I'll see you tonight then, at nine thirty."

"Sure." We hung up and I sat staring at Gallin. Before she could ask me anything I said, "I remember seeing a film many years ago about the adventures of Biggles. He was a First World War RAF pilot."

"I know who Biggles is. I grew up on Biggles, and the Famous Five."

"OK, so there is this guy—or a chap, I should say—who leaves a message for Biggles. I can't remember what is said in the message, but Biggles knows immediately it's a filthy German trap because there is a split infinitive in the message,

'A split infinitive from an Oxford Man!' he scoffs. 'Impossible!'"

"I am sure there is a point to that charming story."

"There is. It's like in *From Russian with Love*, when Bond knows that the Russian agent posing as the British agent Nash is an impostor because he orders red wine with fish."

"That was what made Bond special, before Broccoli's Woke Wankers got to him."

"Quite, let's go meet the gang, I'll explain on the way."

It was a long and winding path that led us eventually to Manassas and from there to State Route 234, going south. The road was broad, but even so you felt yourself enveloped by the superabundance of trees that seemed to billow like dense, green smoke on all sides. Pretty soon we came to Independence Hill and turned right onto Independence Hill Drive. A couple of twists and turns after that took us past the Carolina University of Theology and down Joplin Road, deep into dark woods along Route 619.

This road was not broad and ample, and the trees did not billow like green smoke. This road was narrow and what lay beyond the next bend was obscured by trees that were tall and thin, and seemed to lean across the blacktop, laying long, black shadows in our path.

Gallin said, "I didn't know they'd named a road after her." I glanced at her. "Janis Joplin," she explained.

"Oh."

"Her 'Summertime' ranks with the best. Except for her stupid husband playing medieval guitar in the background."

"Yes."

We moved on through the forest, with the dark road

unfolding before through shadows. We passed a glade on the left with a sign that said Carpet and Upholstery Care. There was something surreal about that. Soon the trees closed in overhead, blocking out the sky, and the light turned green. The road seemed to be never ending.

And then we came to a turnoff on the right and I slowed and turned in. There was a Land Rover there with four Marines in it armed with assault rifles. They jumped down as we pulled in and the sergeant approached me and saluted.

"This is a restricted area, sir. You can't be here."

I pulled my card from my wallet and showed it to him.

"I can, Sergeant. And this is Sergeant Gallin."

She had got out and showed him her ID too.

"Yes, sir. You are expected. Through the barrier, turn right, pass the range and take the send on your left. The facility is half a mile on your right."

They raised the barrier for us and we drove through. A right turn took us even deeper into the forest. We passed the range and at the second intersection turned into what might well have been Tolkien's Mirkwood. The canopy had become so impenetrable the headlamps came on. But after half a mile we came to a wooden gate. Gallin jumped out and opened it, and I rolled through.

It wasn't much to look at. It was a steel prefab. about two stories high and painted in camouflage green, like jungle fatigues. It was surrounded by trees and either had vegetation growing on the roof, or a synthetic canopy. It must have been completely invisible from the air. We had been just a few yards away and we had not seen it from the road.

A door opened in the façade and a Marine stepped out, pointing vigorously to the side of the building, where I now saw a door opened to allow me access to an underground parking garage. He leaned over the door.

"Lot thirty-two."

As we rolled down the ramp Gallin tilted her head on one side and spread her hands.

"See, these are the things you can do when you lose a trillion dollars a year."

I raised an eyebrow at her and spun the wheel, spiraling down into the darkness. The tires screamed and echoed among the caverns.

"You have to stop reading those conspiracy theory websites. It's more than a trillion."

"More."

"You're forgetting the tax the CIA makes the cartels in Mexico and Colombia pay to allow them to stay in business."

I pulled in to lot thirty-two and killed the engine. She opened her door, paused a moment and looked at me. "That's not funny."

"No argument from me."

We crossed through the dingy, echoing shadows toward the warm amber oblong of the elevators. A plate-glass door slid open and a Marine lieutenant stepped out and saluted.

We showed him our ID. He examined them careful and then made a full frank and honest inspection of our faces.

"Please follow me."

He took us up two floors in a large, steel elevator, then out into a passage with cream walls and a beige carpet and round a corner to a door that was barely distinguishable from the wall, except that there was a large, square pad next to it. The Marine put his thumb to the pad and the door hissed open. The architect had obviously been a fan of the Next Generation.

The Marine stepped in ahead of us. Here the carpet was deep blue and the walls were paneled in dark wood. There was a wooden desk. Behind the desk, on the wall, were the Great Seal and the Stars and Stripes, and in a brown leather chair a woman who looked like she ate babies for breakfast. The lieutenant came to attention and said, "Captains Alex Mason and Aila Gallin to see the director."

She pressed a button on her desk and an oblong section of the wall hissed open. We went through.

I don't know what I was expecting, but I wasn't expecting what I saw. Though, knowing Nero as I did, maybe I should have. If I had seen it in a DC comic, as part of Lex Luthor's pad under Gotham City, it would not have surprised me.

It was a large, open space. The floor was a thick, dark blue pile carpet. There were no windows, but one wall had a large aquarium while another had changing 3-D images of landscapes: a Caribbean island, the Wind River Mountains, fall in New England...

There was an open fireplace which at that moment stood cold with a case of orange chrysanthemums in it. Arranged around it were a huge calico sofa and two huge calico chairs. Beside these were low, heavy lamp tables with fat porcelain lamps on them. Elsewhere in the room there were two more nests of chairs and sofas arranged around coffee tables, and there was a long, black dining table on a mezzanine floor with twelve black chairs arranged around it. There were also ferns and palms and rubber plants in gigantic flowerpots.

Nero, huge, was standing in front of the fireplace with his hands behind his back, staring at us. Lounging on the sofa, also looking at us, was a man I recognized as Frank Costello. Beyond them, at one of the nests of chairs and sofas I saw a striking, middle-aged woman in jeans and a plaid shirt. She was talking earnestly, and even urgently to a very long man with a thin face, deep-set eyes and a large nose. He had the kind of angular body that made all clothes look badly cut. He was paying careful attention to his reading glasses, apparently ignoring the woman.

I said, "Sir,"

He said, "Ah, come in. Good." He pointed at the man on the sofa. "Senator Frank Costello, Captains Aila Gallin and Alex Mason. It should be self evident, to a man of your intellect, which is which. Over there are Ms. Priti Anand and Mr. Johannes de Jong. Come in, sit. Will you have a drink?"

We stepped in and the door closed behind us. Anand had turned in her seat to look at us and de Jong had shifted his gaze from his glasses to Gallin.

"No." I made my way toward the seat at the far end of the sofa from Costello. "Thanks. I'd like to get started." I raised my voice. "Ms. Anand, Mr. de Jong, would you like to join us over here?"

Priti Anand sat opposite me in the big armchair, beside Costello who had nestled himself into the corner. De Jong dragged over a chair for Gallin and offered it to her with a smile that was tinged with a leer. She thanked him and he sat next to Costello on the sofa, though there was about an acre between them.

"Senator Costello, have you in the last year or two been

approached by anybody wanting you to lobby for the Russians?"

He gave a big bark of a laugh. "And the Chinese and the North Koreans and the Iranians... Son, the minute you step into Congress, every mother's son who's got a buck to spare wants to give it to you so you will lobby for their special interests, whether it's better care for stray cats or more influence for the damned Kremlin."

I nodded. You can always trust a politician to miss the point and focus on the irrelevant.

"Let me rephrase the question, Senator: during, or before, the suitcase bombings were you approached by anyone who wanted you to play down the importance of a nuclear threat, and stress that the whole thing was a hoax, for example?"

His eyes shifted and he looked down at his shoes and pursed his lips, like he was blowing them a kiss. There was silence. Eventually Nero, standing in front of the cold fireplace still, went up on his toes and boomed: "The consequences for you, for everyone in this room and for the future of this country, are so momentous, Costello—" The use of his bald surname, bordering on the offensive, made the senator look up. Nero went on: "—if you lie, prevaricate or manipulate the truth, that I would have you sectioned and confined if you even contemplate being *anything less than absolutely truthful!*"

His last five words were emitted as a furious roar, which was accompanied by the crimson flushing of his cheeks and a small spray of spittle from his lips.

Costello's eyebrows rose on his forehead and his eyes shifted to me. Maybe he was wondering how much of what

Nero had said was bluster and how much was true. He was wise to wonder.

"Yes," he said. "I was approached."

"By whom, man!"

It was Nero who asked but Costello answered me, like he was hoping I'd take up the questioning again.

"Jerry Feynman. At first his line was that it would cause a crash in the stock market if investors began to panic and pull their money out of the US, and that would be catastrophic for the economy." He shrugged and gave a small laugh. "I reminded him my party was not in government and I couldn't take responsibility for their failed policies. I also told him there might be a damned nuclear device in the country and we should take that seriously."

Gallin asked him, "How did he respond to that?"

Costello looked at her and licked his lips. "It was kind of weird."

"What was?"

He gave another laugh. "I mean politicians, we're like lawyers, right? Everybody assumes we have no morals, no ethics, all we care about is power. And I guess the higher up the hierarchy you go, the more true that becomes. But even in the White House, you know, most people have a kind of basic morality, a point past which they won't go. Most are patriotic, believe in justice and democracy. There is a kind of low bar that most people in politics meet."

Gallin was frowning. "So?"

"So Jerry really, *really* didn't seem to care about the bomb. I mean the nuclear one. He told me it was a hoax, that he could guarantee no Russian terrorist group had a tactical nuclear device. So I asked him, 'OK, what if it's not a terrorist group? What if it's the Kremlin operating through a phony group?'" He paused, his face somewhere between a wince and a smile. He shook his head. "I couldn't believe it. He said, and I remember verbatim because it shook me up so much, 'Look, so Wall Street gets blown to hell, so what? Have you any idea the opportunities that will generate, and how investors will flock to pour money into the collapsing industries? There are no problems, Frank, only opportunities.' I told him to go to hell before I knocked his head off. After that you found the device and it kind of blew over. Tell you the truth, the whole thing was so weird, and Feynman is such a creep, I just put it down to him being weird."

I asked him, "Did he offer you money?"

"Yeah, yeah, he did. He asked me how much it would cost for me to shut up about finding the suitcases. I threatened to call security and he backed off."

Nero said, "I have informed you all that this conversation is being recorded. You understand that?"

"Yeah, yeah, I know."

Priti Anand spoke suddenly. "Are we to understand that Jerry Feynman is behind this hit list?"

I stared at her for a long moment, wondering if I had got the corners of the jigsaw all wrong. "No," I said, "no, he's not."

EIGHTEEN

I turned to Nero. "Maybe I'll have that drink after all." He pressed a button over the fireplace. I turned to de Jong. "Mr. de Jong, had you disclosed to anyone whom you were intending to back for nomination?"

He nodded a few times, examining his reading glasses, before saying, "Yes, of course. Priti and I had discussed it. We had talked it over with a few other people."

"How few is a few?"

"Maybe five or six people. Gates and Zuckerberg after the last Bilderberg gathering, Musk, I talked it over with Don, and Feynman, of course."

"Feynman? Why. He works for the competition."

"Yeah, but DC isn't about politics, Mr. Mason, DC is about power. Senator Costello is known to be a hawk. He is also known for seeing through what he says he is going to do. He is popular and stands a damned good chance of getting in with a majority in the House. That would be very bad news for the opposition. So Jerry wanted us to split our support and back an 'also ran.'"

"Someone with more Russian sympathies."

He made a face and shrugged. "I don't think you'll find many people with real pro-Russian sympathies in Washington these days, but perhaps someone more ready to relax sanctions and negotiate."

"What did you tell Jerry Feynman?"

The door opened and a man in a burgundy uniform stepped in with a tray of decanters, glasses and bottles, and a silver bucket of ice. He set it down on a sideboard and began to unload it. De Jong was saying, "I told him I was going to back Frank. Reed barely had a functioning neuron in his skull. I'm sorry he's disappeared and I hope he's OK, but frankly he did us all a favor. The man had less backbone than a sipuncula and less personality too. Besides, he had this infatuation with all things French, which I always find suspect."

Priti giggled and de Jong winked at her, then carried on. "As to Helen of Troy, she is a crowd pleaser who tries to be all things to all men. If she's in some redneck cowboy state she's all about the Second Amendment, building walls and slashing taxes. But the closer she gets to either coast the more her tune starts to change and suddenly this is the great land of opportunity, wherever you're from, whatever color you are and whatever sexes you may be or have been or intend to be in the future. In Wyoming she is all guns and graft, in New York she's all about supporting Israel and in San Francisco it's important to have an inclusive dialogue with Iran and Saudi to see how we can address their concerns." He took a deep breath and shook his head. "You can't trust a person like that. She's cute, the camera likes her and she's like Obama. They're articulate and make you believe they really mean what they're saying, even when they are lying through their very white teeth. But you can't trust them, because the moment it is in their interest, they will cut your throat and bleed you dry while they explain to you, very eloquently, why it's in your interest." He gestured at Costello. "But Frank will actually commit political suicide sooner than compromise his beliefs."

I eyed Costello a moment and wondered if that was true. Then I turned to Priti Anand.

"Excuse me, sir. Would you like me to prepare the drinks?"

It was the guy in the burgundy uniform. He was addressing Nero. Beside the big man he looked very small, maybe five foot or five two. Nero turned to Priti Anand, "What will you have, Madam?"

"Vodka martini, Sam knows how I like it."

She smiled at the kid and he bowed. Nero turned to Gallin. "Captain."

"Water. No ice, no lemon."

De Jong said, "Beefeater and tonic."

"Bourbon, straight up."

I said, "Bushmills, straight up."

Nero waved his hand at the kid and he went back to the tray to fix the drinks. Anand was still watching me. I met her gaze and asked, "What about you, Ms. Anand?"

"What about me, Mr. Mason?"

"Did you tell anybody about your intentions?"

"My intentions?" She smiled with excessively clear intent, then said, "Pretty much the same as Johannes. I was present at most of those meetings. We work together very closely because we have very similar views."

"You had no meetings with Russian oligarchs, ex KGB or Russian Mafia?"

"I tend to stay clear of the Russians, Mr. Mason. They became a ticking time bomb the moment the Berlin Wall came down, and I told that creep Feynman in no uncertain terms. My money was going to Frank Costello, because he was a man you could trust—not if you were an illegal migrant or a refugee, and not if you were an Iranian planning to make weapons-grade plutonium—but if you were a true patriot, Frank Costello was your man."

Costello gave her the thumbs up. "Thanks, Priti, 'preciate that."

Gallin spoke up again. "So you both let it be known pretty unequivocally that you would be supporting Senator Costello, and why."

They both nodded and de Jong said, "Yup."

I watched absently as the kid approached with a silver tray and handed Anand her drink. She set it on the table beside her and he turned and gave Gallin her water before giving de Jong and Costello theirs. I took my Bushmills from the kid and set it on the table beside me. The kid gave a little bow and left the room.

I glanced at Nero and he shook his big head. "There is nothing here that contradicts what Feynman has told us, and Feynman has admitted to being in the pay of the Russians. But I am very much afraid Feynman is going to be a scapegoat because we have interrogated him and he has no idea who, precisely, he was working for in Moscow."

"Sir, can we have a brief word outside."

"Of course." He turned to the others. "Excuse us a moment."

He led the way across the room to the door which hissed open and we stepped out into the corridor. As the door closed I told him, "Peter Belov, or somebody who claims to be him, called me as we were leaving Senator Troy's place."

He eyes narrowed into needles. "Are you serious? What did he want?"

"He wanted to tell me who was behind all this back in Moscow. He said it was a woman."

"Did he tell you her name?"

"No, he said not on the phone and that he was taking a huge risk."

"Not on the phone? Does he intend you to fly to Belize?"

"No, he claims he's here in DC and wants to meet tonight at nine thirty."

"Where?"

"Seven Locks Road, in Westlake. He says he has a house there."

"Do you trust him?"

"No, sir. I am on that list. I believe it's a trap."

"What do you plan to do?"

I glanced around. "Are we being recorded?"

"No."

"I plan to go there and kill the bastard, and send his head to Putin in the diplomatic bag."

"Figuratively speaking, of course."

"Of course."

"Captain Gallin will go with you?"

"Yes."

"Do you need anybody else?"

"No, I don't want to spook..." As I was speaking we both heard the elevator arrive and now feet were pounding down the corridor. Nero blustered, "Confound it! What is this?"

A Marine sergeant skidded round the corner with two Marines behind him. He was pointing at the door and shouting, *"Ms. Anand's bodyguards! They've been killed!"*

I heard Nero splutter, "What the..." but I was already hammering at the switch to open the door. Nothing was happening and I was preparing to kick the door in when Nero bellowed, "Get out of the way, you fool!" shoved me aside and placed his thumb on the button. The door hissed open and I charged in bellowing, *"Freeze! Don't drink! Glasses down!"* And I was scanning them as I was shouting.

Gallin's glass was on the floor untouched. She was getting to her feet. Priti Anand had her glass in her hand halfway to her mouth. Costello had his nestled in his lap and was staring at me and his companions by turns. De Jong was staring at his half-empty glass.

"Vomit!" I yelled and rushed at him. *"Stick your damned fingers down your throat! Vomit!"* He was standing, bending double, shoving his fingers down his throat and retching. I turned to the Marines and pointed. "You, get warm salt water on the double. Lots of salt! You, get a doctor, fast!" To the sergeant I snarled, "That man has been poisoned. Deal with it." I went to Nero. "Who was the kid? The waiter?"

"Part of Anand's staff. She claimed he was trusted staff."

I looked for Gallin. She was kneeling in front of Anand. I went and hunkered next to her. "Ms. Anand, I am very sorry if you were close to them, but there is no time. Your bodyguards have been murdered."

"No! Akal? Randeep..."

"The waiter. When did you employ him?"

"I don't know. My secretary vets them and looks at their references..."

I had stopped listening and was making for the door, shouting, "Sergeant, with me!" He followed us out to the corridor. I snapped, "Questions: where did you find the bodyguards?"

"In Ms. Anand's quarters, sir!"

"Was there anybody else in her apartments? A young kid in a burgundy uniform, a waiter?"

"No, sir!" The elevator arrived around the corner and a Marine and a doctor ran past. "There was just Ms Anand's personal assistant. She was screaming and hysterical. She found the bodies and called us."

Gallin frowned. "Personal assistant? Personal assistant or secretary?"

He looked nonplussed. "Uh... She said personal assistant."

"Very short, slight, pale, blue eyes..."

"Yeah—"

I exploded, "Goddammit! The waiter! How could I be so stupid! Can she get off the base?" Before he could answer I shouted, "Sound the alarm! Hold anyone leaving the base! Find that girl!"

I ran, with Gallin close on my heels. I ignored the elevator and took the stairs three at a time. Behind me I could hear the sergeant on his radio, giving instructions. By the time we reached the ground floor the place was swarming with men in uniform running for the exit. As I elbowed and shouldered my way through the milling soldiers I saw an officer moving toward me. I noted he had the rank of colonel.

"Stop right there! Who are you?"

I was about to tell him I had no time when Gallin and the sergeant collided with me. The sergeant snapped to attention and saluted.

"Sir! These are Captains Mason and Gallin. Ms. Priti Anand's bodyguards have been murdered, sir, and Mr. de Jong is receiving medical treatment—"

The colonel's face had turned crimson and he bellowed, "On *my* base?"

I pointed at the sergeant. "He will explain. I have a killer to catch!"

"*Go! Goddammit! What are you wasting time for? Go!*"

Gallin didn't need telling twice. By the time he'd finished shouting she was already out the door, and I was right behind her. And what confronted us was the oblong clearing into which we had driven, and a forest so dense you could barely see your hand in front of your face. Here and there teams of Marines were disappearing among the trees, fanning out, calling to each other as they went. Within fifteen seconds they had all disappeared.

I stood and stared. "We just lost maybe fifty men as big as trucks in fifteen seconds, and we want to find one nearly invisible wisp of smoke."

———

Steve had been tidying up while Akal and Randeep played cards. They were having a rest while their mistress was at the meeting with de Jong, Costello and the fat man. The apartment they had given her was pretty good by military standards, though nothing like what she was accustomed to. There was an all-in-one kitchen, dinner and living room that had no windows and only one door. So escape, if one wanted to escape, was impossible.

That thought had made him smile.

Sally, Anand's PA or secretary or whatever the hell she was, was lying under Anand's bed with a broken neck. He had left her eyes open because it amused him to think of her lying in that dark space staring wide-eyed at the wooden slats, seeing nothing. That had been just before the big meeting, which had been delayed because Mason was late.

As soon as Anand had gone, the two giant Sikhs had sat down to play cards and he had set about tidying up. Occasionally he glanced at them, calibrating how aware they were of him, how accustomed to his moving about, and how deeply involved in their game. He knew his window of opportunity was small because soon they would want their drinks. The Sikhs had to be dead before that happened.

He took a couple of glasses to the kitchen area and picked up a medium-sized slicing knife he had sharpened earlier, and the smaller vegetable knife. With no pause in his movements he returned to the dining area, where the two men were at the table, facing each other, absorbed in their cards and, again without pause, he approached them, reached out and thrust the two blades into the side of their necks, severing their carotid arteries and their aortas.

They gaped at each other, reached for the handles of the

knives, and at that point he levered the blades inward. By then the massive loss of blood to the brain had become catastrophic. They lost consciousness and died almost immediately and fell forward onto the table. There had been very little spray because he had not removed the blades, but now blood oozed copiously over the table and the cards.

In his room he had already prepared the girl's clothes he would wear, so all he had to do then was sit and wait for the call to bring the drinks. The tray with the decanters and the glasses was ready in the kitchen. Each glass he had smeared with a concentrated essence of aconite.

The call had come soon afterwards. It had amused him to open the door and back out of the apartment carrying the tray, and for a few seconds to have the two dead Sikhs, with their turbans and their astonished faces flat on the table, in full view.

The drinks had gone without a hitch. He had noticed Mason looking at him briefly, but he had soon lost interest. He knew Mason had not drunk his whiskey. He had heard his voice shouting when they had started the search. That was OK. Steve always had a backup plan, and he would get Mason later. He smiled. In any case, the others at least were by now dead.

He could hear the apes tramping through the trees and the ferns below. He knew without any doubt that all of their attention would be focused on the dense growth of ferns. It would not occur to them that he might have climbed into the canopy. The trees were tall and straight, and the branches did not start until a height of eight or ten feet.

He'd had a head start of a couple of minutes. Steve was a fast sprinter and he had lost himself among the trees long before they had given the alarm. Climbing into the canopy had been a simple matter of using a long strip of rubber slung around the trunk and his waist, and inching his way up. It had taken him no more than fifteen seconds to reach the first branches. By the time he'd heard the first shouts he was already invisible, high among the top branches, motionless and silent. Within the hour they would assume he had made it to the road and, dressed as a girl as he was, had managed to get a ride from some passing car.

And they would be right, but that would be later, later this afternoon. He would find a driver hoping for some erotic fun. He would grant their wish. He smiled and closed his eyes, slowing his breathing and entering a mild trance. He would give them the ride of their life. The last ride of their life.

NINETEEN

SOME FIVE HOURS LATER IT WAS MIDNIGHT IN Moscow, but Colonel Alexandrina Vitsin was still at her desk in her small, dark office overlooking Mokhovaya Street. She had the stub of a rollup pinched in her fingers and was attempting to suck the last bit of smoke from it without burning her fingers.

Her telephone rang and she saw from the screen that it was Steve. She answered and could hear a television in the background.

"Report."

"I am at the house in Westlake, watching the news. It seems Senator Frank Costello, financier Priti Anand and entrepreneur Johannes de Jong have all died in a freak poisoning accident."

She dragged her breath through the coagulated nicotine and tar in her throat in something that started out as a laugh but ended up as a happy coughing fit.

"You are my *dorogoy* boy. You were always the best."

"I am nothing, *mumiya*. You are everything. I exist for you."

She smiled and sighed. There was real pleasure in the sound. He spoke again.

"There was a fat man. I don't know who he was, but he seemed to be in charge of the investigation. I think he was Mason's boss. He is not mentioned in the news report, but I know he is not dead because he did not drink. But he was not on the list. Also, Mason has a partner, an Israeli woman called Captain Aila Gallin. She was not on the list. She asked for water, but she did not drink."

"That is fine. What about Mason?"

"I will kill him tonight."

"Good, my *dorogoy* boy, always so good. Soon you can come home and have a nice rest. You will like that, won't you, dear Stephan?"

"Yes, *mumiya*. I will like that."

"And we can play our sweet games. You miss our sweet games, Stephan?"

"Yes, *mumiya*, I only like to play sweet games with you."

"That's my good boy. Call me tonight, when the job is done."

"I will, *mumiya*."

———

AT THAT VERY MOMENT IT was ten past five in the afternoon in Washington DC. In her imitation Oval Office in her home in Great Falls, like Steve, Helen Troy was watching the news channel. She saw that Frank was dead, and Priti and Johannes. She had liked all three of them, in particular she had been fond of Frank. He had reminded her in some ways of Paul. He was honest—to the extent any politician is truly honest—and he'd had good values. She would miss seeing him around town. She would miss plotting and planning with him. She would miss his earthy wisdom.

A voice in her head which she tried to ignore told her she now had no competitors for nomination. And if her growing popularity continued, she had an excellent chance of making it to president at the next elections. Her father's dream. And she liked to think that Paul would be proud of her. Even if toward the end he had disapproved of some of her foreign policy ideas. He had still loved her.

She stood and walked to the tall windows behind her desk, which overlooked the lawns at the front of her house. She could see the Secret Service car there, and as she watched she saw another car pull up. Through the window she could see Captain Gallin's face. She assumed the insufferable Alex Mason was in the car with her. They would be there all night. For a moment she longed for the whole thing to be over. She longed for her family to be installed in the White House, she longed for the Oval Office and her team, working systematically through her agenda for the country. She smiled at the copper light on the road, and the long shadows of the trees. She would leave the country a better place than she had found it. She knew the people would love her. She would be one of the few presidents who were remembered with affection by the nation: George Washington, Abe Lincoln, Franklin D. Roosevelt, JFK and Helen M. Troy. That, her father would have said, was a worthy aspiration.

A worthy aspiration.

He didn't know, couldn't know, would never know because he was dead, how lonely power was. Or how lonely the pursuit of power was.

The shadows grew longer as she stood there, almost unaware of the passage of time. She saw a Jeep pull up and a man climb out. She saw Captain Gallin and Mason get out of their car and the three stood and spoke for a while. Then the captain and the newcomer got into the car and Mason took the Jeep and drove away. She noticed all this as though she were in a trance. It meant nothing to her.

Eventually she returned to her desk and sat, staring at the documents she had in front of her but without seeing them. Instead she saw Jerry, and heard his voice in her head, the last time he had spoken to her. Paul had been right about him. Paul was always right.

Had been always right. Now he was dead.

What Helen Troy did not see was how ten minutes after Mason had driven away in the Jeep, a dark Audi had pulled up behind Captain Gallin's car. The captain had climbed out and made her way to the driver's door. For a moment she had talked through the open window, then opened the door and the driver had got out. He had got into the driver's seat of Captain Gallin's car and she had climbed into the Audi. She had turned it around and driven away at speed.

But Senator Troy had seen none of that. Shortly afterwards, as the dusk quickened toward evening, her maid tapped at the door and poked her head in.

"Dinner is ready, ma'am."

She nodded and smiled. "Thank you, Lucia. I'll be right there."

She rose, put her files in her safe, locked it, made her way to the door and opened it.

———

AT THAT VERY MOMENT, less than a hundred yards away, the man stepped out from among the trees. He stood a moment looking at the house where the drapes had been closed a moment before, shutting in the warm light. He crossed the lawn at a rapid walk, with his hands deep in the pockets of his jacket, and his collar drawn up about his face, even though the evening was balmy. He crossed the driveway and stepped out onto the sidewalk. He continued to walk quickly, like he was in a hurry to get somewhere.

The first car he came to was the car Gallin had recently vacated. He stepped off the sidewalk, hunkered down and pulled the suppressed Glock from under his arm. He hunkered down so he could see the outline of the driver and the passenger through the rear window. He took aim and fired. The subsonic rounds shattered the glass and punched through the skulls of the Mossad agent in the driver's seat and the ODIN agent in the passenger seat beside him. The low velocity rounds made no exit wound but lodged inside the skulls of the two men, tearing their brains to shreds and killing them instantly.

The two Secret Service men in the car fifteen paces away were frowning, staring at the ODIN car. They had noticed the man walk behind the car and disappear. They had noticed the driver and his companion seem to slump. The driver was just asking, "Am I imagining things, or..."

But he got no further. The big man in the jacket

emerged again over the roof of the car. The streetlamp behind him cast an eerie hallow around him, making it hard to see precisely what he was doing. What he was doing was taking aim at the vague forms of the two men who were squinting at him. He double-tapped twice, shattering the windshield and punching two holes in each of their chests. Death did not come so swiftly to them. The tall man walked quickly to their car. The driver had his hand on the door, attempting to open it. The man shot him first, between the eyes. Then he shot his partner. After that he made his way down the path toward the front door of the house.

He paused at the door for a moment, doing something with the lock. Then the door opened inward, revealing the warm light of the entrance hall. Then the door closed. Moments later a sound like firecrackers erupted from the house. There was a scream and more shots rattled in the house. Then pandemonium broke loose. Children screamed and women screamed and a male voice rose above the others. The three tall windows in Senator Troy's office exploded in a sparkling shower of glass. There were more screams. Lights came on upstairs and there were more shots. Then a man's voice roared and moments later the kitchen door at the back of the house burst open and a big man hurtled out into the night, running frantically for the cover of the trees from which he had originally emerged.

Far off the sound of police sirens wailed across the night. It was not long before the pulsing blue and red lights swarmed into the street from both sides and converged on the senator's house. Four patrol cars screeched to a halt and armed police officers spilled from the vehicles, training their weapons on the house.

The front door opened and Senator Helen Troy's body-guard, Isileli Manu, stepped out onto the porch. His shirt was drenched with blood. A cop screamed at him, "*Freeze! Put your hands where I can see them!*"

Manu's face was twisted, distorted with grief. He pointed toward the open door, his mouth sagged open and he fell to his knees. A terrible howl emerged from his lips as he covered his face with his hands.

Two cops stayed with him as the others climbed the stairs to enter the house. They got as far as the door and stopped. One of them turned away and covered his mouth. Sergeant Collins in the lead whispered, "Sweet Jesus..." After a moment he took his radio and called dispatch.

"We are at Senator Helen Troy's house, responding to a ten-thirty-one, possible ten-thirty-two, but," he shook his head, "what we have here is...," he faltered, "it's a massacre. We need at least two ambulances, we need crime scene officers, we need a detective here. I don't know what the hell has happened. I don't know if there are any survivors, but we urgently need medics here, now. This is a slaughterhouse."

He turned to Isileli Manu. "Did you do this?"

The bodyguard just sobbed and shook his head. "I was her protector," he said, "May God forgive me, I was here to protect her family..."

"Sergeant..."

Collins turned. Wells was pointing out toward the road. "Those two cars, the rear window is smashed on the nearest, and the windshield is smashed on the farthest. But, I think I can see people in them."

"What the hell...? You and Jones go check it out. Use *extreme* caution. Chavez, you stay here with this guy, see if you can make any sense of what he's saying. The rest of you come with me. We are looking for survivors. Touch nothing."

The first body they found was Lucia's. She had been shot in the face with a forty-five and the hallway floor was awash with her blood. In the senator's study they found the two cream sofas shot to shreds, as though with an automatic rifle. The desk was shot to matchwood, and the glass in the windows was completely shattered. But there were no bodies, and no sign of the senator.

In the dining room they found the children, eight and ten, shot several times at close range. There was also a young woman, maybe an au pair or a personal assistant. She was lying half sprawled over the children, as though her last act in this world had been to protect them. She had been shot in the stomach, in her shoulder and in the side of her head.

In the passage between the dining room and the kitchen they found the cook, a woman in her fifties, shot five times in the chest and belly. They continued their search upstairs. They found two bedroom doors that had been kicked in, and the wardrobes sprayed with automatic fire. The beds too had been sprayed. In the master bedroom there was a similar scene. The wardrobe here was vast and had sliding full-length mirrors as doors. These had been shattered by gunfire and huge pieces of glass lay strewn across the floor, the wooden backing peppered with holes.

A small noise led Sergeant Collins to step across the glass and slide open the doors. The senator was there, on the floor, curled into the fetal position, trembling and sobbing. After a moment she raised her face and looked up at Collins. She was sickly pale and had vomited on the floor.

"Senator Troy?" She didn't answer at first. Outside he could hear the ambulances arriving, along with the ME and the crime scene officers. He said again, "Are you Senator Helen Troy?"

She nodded, and her voice was barely a whisper. "Yes, my children, he killed..."

She trailed off and made an ugly wailing noise, and Collins reached down for her. "Come on, let's get you out of here."

He took a coat from the wardrobe and wrapped her in it. He knew she was in shock and would soon start trembling with cold. He guided her down the steps, holding her face against his shoulder so she wouldn't see the maid and the cook, out onto the porch from where he led her to one of the ambulances.

"Is there anyone we can call? Anyone to be with you?"

Her lower lip was trembling. She shook her head in small, short jerks. "They're all dead," she said. "All of them. They are all dead."

A tall man in a suit with no tie crossed the law toward them. He jerked his head at the sergeant. "Sergeant Collins?"

"Yes, Detective."

He turned to the senator. "Are you Senator Helen Troy?"

"Yes."

"Detective Joe Brown, MPD. I am very sorry for your loss, ma'am. You look like you need to get to a hospital and have the doctors look you over. Is there anything you can tell me? Anything at all that might help?"

Her eyes glazed. "He was big, silent. He had a balaclava or something over his face. But his hands. I saw his hands and they were white. I think he was wearing latex gloves. He just stormed in while we were eating." She faltered, then, "Isileli was upstairs. It was so sudden and unexpected. So confusing. I was trying to protect the children. But they wee already... And Isileli came charging in. They fought. Isileli dragged me and told me to go upstairs and hide in the wardrobe. I heard screaming and shouting and gunfire. Then the wardrobe seemed to explode with noise and the doors shook. And I don't know what happened after that." She looked back at the sergeant. "Is Isileli...? Did he...?"

Collins shook his head. "He's OK. He's traumatized and in shock. He feels he's betrayed you."

"He saved my life."

Detective Brown nodded. "OK, let's get you to the hospital. Is there anybody we can call?"

She hesitated, about to give him the same answer she had given Collins moments before, but instead said, "Yes. Alex Mason. He tried to protect me. He's with the Office of the Director of Intelligence Networks. He needs to be informed, and I would like to talk to him."

Detective Brown nodded. "I'll see to it."

TWENTY

I PULLED INTO ROSEHILL DRIVE OF SEVEN LOCKS Road at twenty minutes past nine. I had told Gallin I needed her at Senator Troy's house. We had put out a misleading press release stating that Priti Anand and Costello had both been poisoned and they and de Jong were dead. De Jong was critical and Anand and Costello were under close observation at the base, but the fact was that his extremely ambitious and daring attempt had failed.

However, right then he believed the only names left on his list were Senator Troy's and mine. And that made him extremely dangerous, and it made Senator Troy a prime target.

But that wasn't the reason I had told Gallin to stay with her. The reason was much more simple, and much more stupid than that. I knew that the killer's next target was me. I knew because he had told me. He had told me to come to this house tonight at nine thirty. He'd done that because he knew, whether I believed his story about being Peter Belov or not, I would have to come.

And I had come to realize also that this killer was subtle beyond anything I had encountered before. He seemed to be quite fearless, and his fearlessness made him unpredictable. And that made him very, very dangerous. And *that* was the reason I had told Gallin to stay with Troy.

I was aware that made me an egotistical male chauvinist who undervalued strong women, but I didn't really care. What mattered to me was that I got a chance to neutralize this bastard before he got too close to Gallin. After that they could try me for crimes against Wokery and hang me from the neck till I Woke up. Just so long as Gallin was safe.

The professional side of my mind was telling me I was being stupid and that I needed an agent of Gallin's caliber to back me up right then. But the professional side of my mind was free to go take a flying...

The house was large and set back from the road among well-kept lawns flanked on all sides by large pines, mainly of the Christmas tree variety. There were also other types of trees which I couldn't identify in the dark, but they effectively cut the house off from view.

I had pulled up opposite the drive and sat watching the house for a couple of minutes. I saw no movement and no lights, but that of itself didn't mean much. So I spun the wheel and pulled across the road into the drive and parked outside the double garage. I climbed out of the roadster and crossed the lawn to the five steps that led to the porch.

Nobody shot me and nobody jumped out to stab me in the back. So far so good.

I knocked softly at the door, and when nothing

happened I rang the bell. Nothing happened then either. So I walked to the end of the veranda, dropped down to the lawn and made my way to the back of the house. There I found a paved patio area with a built-in barbeque, a white, wrought-iron table with four chairs, and a couple of deck chairs.

A couple of shallow steps led from the paved patio down to the lawn, which was, like the front of the house, screened by tall pines.

Access from the house to the patio was via sliding, plate-glass doors, one of which was open about four inches. I had a mental flash of Colonel Paul Hirschfield's house when Gallin and I entered in the same way.

I pulled the Sig Sauer from under my arm, moved to the left of the porch and flattened myself against the wall. Then I very slowly, silently, inched my way toward the opening. When I could reach out and touch it, I hunkered down into a squat, took a hold of the door and slid it back.

Nothing happened.

Still in a squat, I took a big step to the far side of the opening, stood and peered into the room. There wasn't much to see, except darkness. So I pushed the door a little farther open, hunkered down again and slipped inside with the P226 held out in front of me in both hands. I covered every angle of the room, and still didn't get shot. The fact didn't make me feel any more relaxed. Instead it gave me the feeling he had known in advance every step I was going to take; and with every predictable step I took I was moving deeper into a trap.

I swore softly under my breath and moved to the door. It opened soundlessly inward. I hunkered down again and peered round the doorjamb into a broad hallway that was softly illuminated by the streetlamps that were filtered through the glass panels in the front door.

I moved into the hall, pressed against the wall beside the door, in the shadows, and waited, listening. There was a sound, soft, on the edge of hearing. I slowed my breathing and tried to focus, but it was impossible to locate.

Then there was a voice, quiet, making no effort to be heard. It said, "I'm in the dining room."

I inched along the wall and came to the next door. It was ajar and I reached over and pushed gently. It opened inward. I stepped in with the gun held out in front of me, in both hands.

He was at the far end of the room, sitting in darkness, with his hands laid flat on the table in front of him, He was pale, almost luminous in the shadows, but his eyes were like two dark holes watching me. He spoke again and again his voice was very quiet.

"Come in, Mr. Mason. Please, sit down and let's talk."

"You are not Peter."

There was no expression on his face. "You met Peter?"

"Briefly, but I didn't need to see you to know you're not him."

"Really? Deduction? What did I do wrong?"

I smiled. "For a start you didn't drawl. It's a class thing. People like Peter drawl. You wouldn't know how. You also split your infinitive. Peter would never have done that."

He gave a funny little giggle. "I split my infinitive?"

I recited, "Yeah, you said, 'It would be a shame to stupidly screw things up.' You split the infinitive 'to screw' by stupidly putting stupidly in the middle. A man of Peter's class would not have done that."

"I'll make sure to remember that. So, if you knew I was not Peter, why did you come?"

"To interrogate you and, if I don't kill you, to arrest you."

"Oh," he said, like it made sense. "Do you realize that even as we speak, you are dying?"

I felt my skin go cold and the hairs on the back of my neck prickle. "What are you talking about?"

"If you knew I was not Peter, you must have known my purpose in having you come here was to kill you. The moment you opened the living-room door to step into the hall you started to absorb a synthesized form of curare, which is designed to be absorbed through the skin."

I moved toward the table, pulled out the chair and sat. "That's how you killed Paul."

"With him it was a small dart shot into his neck. It is faster acting than when absorbed through the skin."

"I recognize you. You were the waiter at the facility."

"Most people don't even notice me. I am transparent, unless I become a girl. Then some men find me attractive."

"Like Senator Reed."

"Dirty old man."

"What's to stop me shooting you right now?"

He smiled. There was something horrific about the expression, with his eyes like black holes in his face.

"I doubt you'd have the strength in your hands to pull the trigger. It is too late now to reverse the effects, and you probably hope to keep me talking so that I might tell you who sent me, who employed me, why I am doing this. I know your type, Mr. Mason."

I licked my lips. I didn't feel great. My lips felt fat, like I'd been to the dentist and had a shot.

"OK, so give a dying man a last cigarette. Who's back in Moscow, pulling the strings?"

His laugh was a high-pitched giggle. "Please. You think this is going to be like one of those stupid movies, where the bad guy tells all just before the good guy has a miraculous escape and kills the bad guy? I'm afraid not, Mr. Mason. When you are too weak to resist, I will shove your Sig Sauer in your mouth and use your finger to press the trigger. I am not going to explain anything to you."

I tried to say, "Jerry," but it came out, "Zjelly, Fnm..."

"Jerry Feynman? What about him?"

"Chalking, sh...shalking..."

"You're pathetic."

He stood and came around the table. He took hold of my wrist and lifted it, then let my hand drop to the table. I noticed the P226 was lying on the table in front of me, but there was absolutely nothing I could do to take a hold of it.

He reached out, took hold of the weapon and fitted it into my right hand, closed my fingers on the butt and slipped my finger into the trigger guard. Then he bent my arm around to press the cannon into my mouth. I tried to clamp my teeth, but couldn't, tried to shout but could barely get enough breath in my lungs.

"Don't try to resist, Mr. Mason. I promise you, the death from asphyxia which is the eventual outcome of this drug is far more distressing and unpleasant than a quick, short, sharp shot."

He got the barrel past my teeth, holding my hand with both of his, and carefully adjusted the angle of the shot.

"We want it to penetrate the brain and kill you instantly. Some people make a real mess of this, rip out half the neck and the tongue but survive. We don't want that." He said it matter-of-factly, like he was teaching me how to kill people this way. "OK, so let's get this done."

I felt the pressure of his finger on mine and knew that I had failed. It had been a gamble, but it had not paid off. He had, in the end, outsmarted me.

That was when I heard the loud *clack* and the front door shook slightly. He removed the Sig from my mouth and laid my hand and the gun on the table in front of me. I heard myself make a small sound of relief. He moved to the dining-room door, which was still ajar, and I heard the front door open. My hand was on the table, lying there like it was somebody else's. I could only move my eyes, and breathing was becoming a real struggle. I looked down and saw my watch, and calculated I had been in the house close to fifteen minutes. I had touched the living-room door maybe six or seven minutes earlier.

Sudden scuffling noise came to me from the hall. A grunt, violent exhalations, a crash of furniture. Six minutes. I breathed in and out a few times as hard as I could and pushed with my legs. It was like trying to unbend boiled leather. The chair fell back with a clatter and I was left half-frozen like an upended letter L.

In the hall a woman snarled. I heard the smack and thud of punches. More furniture fell and a vase crashed. I started inching my way like a hundred-year-old man toward the door. There was a loud thud: the sound of a heavy body hitting the floor, and then the sound of dragging—somebody dragging a body across the floor.

My heart started to pound hard. I tottered and almost fell. I reached the door with a fire of adrenaline in my belly, but could not close my fingers on the handle. I got my elbow in the crack and squeezed through.

There was nothing in the hall but limpid light from the streetlamps outside, an overturned coat stand and a broken vase of flowers. I could hear my heart pounding in my ears so hard it was rocking my body. Down the hall, toward the kitchen I could see a door in the wall that was open. Orange-yellow light reflected on the wall, and I knew it was the cellar.

Half a dozen tottering steps got me across the floor to the door and I looked in. There was a flight of wooden steps running down a bare brick wall. At the bottom I could see a concrete floor, a washer, a stack of cartons and a pile of old furniture, a drier and in the middle of the floor a furnace. Between the bottom of the steps and the furnace door Gallin lay spread-eagled on her back. My heart jolted violently in my chest and my belly burned hot.

Two or three paces from her was the pallid young man. He had a trolley, like a gurney, which he was wheeling over to where Gallin lay. I staggered forward and half stumbled down the first step. Somehow I was able to hold on to the rough, pine banister to stop myself falling.

He looked up and saw me. He stood a moment, staring, then collapsed the gurney and hunkered down to roll Gallin onto it. I stumbled down another half-dozen steps and rammed a splinter the size of a small tree into the heel of my hand.

He jacked up the gurney and stood looking at me for a moment, smiling.

"You're a very strong man, Mr. Mason. You should be practically dead. I don't know how you are able to breathe, let alone walk." He smiled, as though he intended to be reassuring. "However, these will soon be moot points, just as soon as I have disposed of Captain Gallin."

I stumbled another couple of steps or three. I could feel warm blood on my left hand from the splinter. The pain was excruciating, but all I could think about was that he was wheeling Gallin toward the furnace. I was looking for blood on the floor where she'd been lying, or wounds on her body, but I couldn't see any. All I could see was a bruise on her jaw. He was going to put her in the furnace alive.

He had reached the furnace door and placed the gurney in front of it. I lowered myself so I was sitting on the steps and steadied my arms on the banister. He hauled the lever and opened the furnace door. There was a roar of sound and blast of hot air. He backed up a step and I took aim with the Sig which he had fixed in my hand. My focus was poor and I barely had the strength to hold the pistol, but I lined him up and squeezed the trigger. The gun exploded and the slug hit him in the right shoulder. He screamed a high-pitched scream and staggered forward, up against the open furnace door. Next thing his clothes were gushing smoke and with a *whoosh!* they were in flames and he was staggering backwards, knocking the gurney out of the way, beating himself with his hands and screaming hysterically.

I dragged myself to my feet and half-fell the rest of the way down the stairs. Somehow I managed the three paces to the gurney. The weird kid had collapsed unconscious among the cartons and the old furniture, and I could see a glimmer of small flames among dense smoke. I began to panic and started slapping Gallin's face.

"Come on baby! Come on, wake up! We still have to buy that ranch and raise fifteen kids, remember?"

She moaned and stirred. Thick black smoke was starting to billow from where the weird kid had fallen and gather under the ceiling. I shook her as frantically as I could and slapped her face. "*Come on, baby! Don't do this to me! I'm not leaving you, you hear! Get up!*"

She made an ugly "Ungh!" noise and I dragged the gurney to the steps. Somehow I got one arm under her and dragged her off the trolley. It spun and tipped over and she fell against me. The black smoke was blocking out the light from the bulb now and growing denser by the moment. I pulled Gallin's arm over my shoulder and hollered as I dragged her up the first step. I yelled again, with each step, "*I —will—not—leave—you—here! I cannot be without you!*"

When I got to the sixth step I heard the whoosh of flames behind me as the old sofa and chars ignited. We still had another eight or ten steps to go, and they were all uphill. But as I dragged her up the next I felt her stir and move and she began to climb with me.

We half ran, half stumbled to the front door, I wrenched it open and we staggered out into the cool night air and collapsed, sprawling on the lawn.

TWENTY-ONE

She sat with her head on my shoulder and I pulled my cell from my pocket. My numb, sausage fingers just about managed nine-one-one but when the operator asked what my emergency was all I could say was, "Ffah... ffah..."

"Sir, what is your emergency?"

"Fff...ffah..."

"Sir, are you swearing at me? Have you got a genuine emergency?"

Gallin was squinting at me. I handed her the phone and pointed to the black smoke that was creeping out of the door. She took the phone.

"We have a fire on Seven Locks Road. The fire is in the basement."

She hung up and handed me the phone. "They're on their way. What is wrong with you? What were you saying on the stairs? You were making these weird noises."

I found I could nod. I thought I'd try for "the waiter."

"Nwaya..."

"You're drugged." I nodded again. "Do you know what he gave you?" I nodded some more. "What?"

"Oo-ah-eh..."

I made the motion of an injection, then just about managed to put my fingers to my head and blow my brains out. She stood.

"Come on, we're going to the hospital. I'll call Nero on the way."

She helped me to the roadster and we pulled out with a screech of brakes onto the road. After a moment I said, "I..."

"What?"

"I," I started again, "cu-ra-re."

"He gave you *curare?* Why aren't you dead?"

"I thon't need a 'ospishl."

"You don't. You were poisoned with curare but you don't need a hospital because you are the Hulk."

I took a deep breath and started to feel a good tingling in my lips and my arms and legs. "I chook an antidote, before going."

"Son of a bitch!"

"The ad...adrenaline and accelerated pulse helped to activate the antidote, which blocked the action of the curare. Eventually."

"Hell, Mason! You should have told me!"

"I told you not to come."

"Good job I ignored you, wasn't it?"

I was silent for a while, then said, "Yes."

"You're welcome."

"He could have killed you, Gallin. He was going to put you in the furnace alive."

"Hot."

"It's not funny."

"Is that what you were saying going up the stairs?"

I shrugged. "I don't remember."

"It sounded like '*Ah blub nyosh bulbj josh ha.*'"

"Then that's probably what I said."

She smiled at me. It was a surprisingly nice smile and I had to look away.

"We need to go to Senator Troy's house."

"Now? You should see a doctor."

"I'll see a doctor afterwards. We need to go there and tell her it's over."

"OK."

I closed my eyes and felt the cool breeze on my face. For a moment, while he was forcing the gun into my mouth, I had known I was going to die. I had not felt fear. I had felt mild surprise, a sense of "Oh, so this is how it happens." But when I had seen what he intended to do with Gallin... My eyes snapped open and I realized I had been asleep.

She glanced at me. "You OK?"

"Yeah. How about you?" I frowned. "He knocked you out?"

She gave me a lopsided smile. "Son of a bitch was fast, and made of elastic. I didn't expect it and he caught me by surprise."

"That weedy little kid."

"Just goes to show. Things are not always what they seem."

We saw the lights before we got there, the red and blue pulse in the air above the trees. As we pulled in, I was staring at the house, crowded with people, the front lawn floodlit and several gurneys on the drive with body bags on them. There were three ambulances, a crime scene van and several patrol cars.

But I noticed Gallin was staring straight ahead. I followed her line of sight and saw the two cars, with police tape around them, the nearest with a shattered rear window and the farthest with the shattered windshield. Both empty.

"What the hell happened here?"

We climbed out and a police sergeant was crossing the lawn toward us. "Sir, ma'am, you can't park here. This is a crime scene."

"I'm Alex Mason," I showed him my card, "this is Captain Gallin. We actually have jurisdiction over this investigation. What has happened here?"

"Alex Mason? I'm Sergeant Collins. I was the first responder. She was asking for you, sir."

"Who, the senator?"

"Yes sir. She was about the only one left. Her and her bodyguard. It was a massacre, sir. They killed the maid, the cook, even the kids and the au pair."

"Who did it?"

"We're still gathering the statements. We were called by several neighbors who said they'd heard screaming and what sounded like firecrackers. We got here in a couple of minutes, but by then it was all over. Seems he was a big guy in a balaclava. The senator said she saw his hands and they were white. Looks like he killed the bodyguards in the car first, then went inside. They were having dinner. He shot the maid in the hall, then the cook, then went into the dining room. By that time," he consulted his notebook, "Isileli Manu, her bodyguard, had come down. Seems they fought and he told her to go upstairs and hide. She hid in the wardrobe in her bedroom and the killer managed to chase her upstairs and spray the wardrobe with automatic fire. Only she was lying on the floor in the fetal position, otherwise he would have killed her. Bodyguard was right behind him. Threw him down the stairs and he fled. We're combing the area for him now."

"You said she wanted to see me?"

"She asked for you specifically."

"Where is she?"

"They wanted to take her to the hospital for observation, but she refused. She is one tough lady. She said she just wanted to go to her apartment on...," he flipped through his notepad, "N Street northwest. James Apartments."

He gave me the exact address and I went inside to inspect the house and have a word with the forensics team. I had a look around her office, at the dining room and the wardrobe upstairs. The last person I spoke to before I left was the ME, who was just wrapping up and getting ready to leave.

I asked him, "How many weapons did he use? Three?"

He pointed at the front door. "Suppressed 9mm out in the cars. Good, accurate shot. An assault rifle in the office and upstairs in the bedroom, and in the dining room he used an assault rifle and a .45 semi-automatic. He was not shy about leaving evidence."

Gallin nodded. "No, he was making a statement. He shot up her office and she wasn't even in there."

I grunted. "Yeah, he wanted to tell us something all right. OK, let's go talk to her."

In the car, as we cruised toward Massachusetts Avenue, she said, "So there were two killers all along."

"Yeah, this is the same guy who killed Dolly."

"Huh." She took her hands off the wheel so she could spread them while she nodded. "So the senator's name was underscored because while the small, freaky guy took care of everybody else, this big guy was going to take care of the senator. All his killings have been related to her, and trying to assassinate her."

"He's not very good though. If she was their prime target they would have been better off doing it the other way around."

"Yeah, this guy is a bit of a brute, right?"

"A very inconsistent brute."

We managed to find a space outside, parked and crossed the mahogany and brass lobby to the elevators under the disapproving gaze of a uniformed porter. We rode the elevator to the ninth floor, trod a sage, patterned carpet illuminated by small, wall-mounted brass lamps, and rang her bell.

The door was opened by Mega Man, whose eyes were very red and swollen.

"I'm here to see the senator," I said.

He nodded, looked away, put a sodden handkerchief to his mouth and screwed up his eyes. After a moment he stepped aside and motioned us to his right. As I stepped in I pulled a clean handkerchief from my pocket and handed it to him. He stared at it a moment. I made a sympathetic face and patted him on the arm. He took the clean handkerchief and I accepted the old wet one.

We moved through a small entrance hall with parquet floors, a mirror and a hat stand which doubled as an umbrella stand, to white double doors with small, stained-glass panels in them. Man Mountain had lumbered away toward the bedrooms, so Gallin knocked and, when there was no reply, she opened the doors and we went in.

The room was a chunky L, and we had entered at the top. The top was a dining area, with an elegant mahogany table set with six chairs and a silver candelabra. To the right the room made a dogleg into a broad area with a terrace and large windows with panoramic views of the city. There were low bookcases along the walls, and eclectic armchairs and sofas scattered apparently at random, flanked by lamp tables with fat lamps. Somehow it worked.

Sitting with her feet curled under her in one of those armchairs was Helen Troy. She was staring out of her huge windows, and didn't look at us as we came in. I felt a stab of irritation but suppressed it. Gallin crossed the room and stood in front of her.

"Anything we say," she said quietly, "will be empty compared with what you are feeling. We are so sorry."

Helen looked up at her and nodded. I saw she had a handkerchief in her hand which she kept folding and unfolding. But unlike Isileli's, this one was dry. Her eyes were not puffy and her nose was not swollen. All her emotions were battened down inside.

She glanced over at me, like she had heard my thoughts. "Mr. Mason, you must be very angry with me."

"Must I?"

"You warned me. I should have listened."

"It was a judgment call. Only about half of those play out right."

She looked back at Gallin. "Please do sit down. Can I get you a drink? I'm having bourbon and valium."

Gallin sat in a big leather chair under the plate-glass window and I sat in an overstuffed calico affair opposite Troy. Gallin said:

"That probably seems like a good idea right now, but you might regret it tomorrow."

"Tomorrow..." She said it like she'd heard about it, but had stopped believing it was real. She shifted her gaze to me. "There is no one left."

"I know."

"What are you when you have no family?" I didn't even try to answer, but she didn't really want me to. She told me, "You're alone. No one to wake you up in the morning. No one to put you to bed. No one to make demands on you, no one you have a right to expect things from. Just the emptiness of a world filled only with you."

Gallin said, "We have some questions. Do you feel up to answering them now?"

She nodded. "I won't feel any better tomorrow. We may as well do it now while the events are fresh."

"Any time you want to stop, you just say so." The senator didn't say anything so Gallin went on. "You were having dinner."

"Yes. I had been in my study. Lucia came in to say dinner was ready. I went to the dining room. The kids were there with Samantha, the au pair. We sat. We chatted for a moment, I can't remember what about. Then I heard the front door open."

I asked, "You didn't hear anything before that? Firecrackers, reports of some kind?"

"No, I just heard the door open. Then a moment later Lucia screamed and there were shots."

Gallin leaned forward. "Please think very carefully about this. How long transpired between those shots and the gunman entering the dining room?"

She sighed and gazed at the glass, where her ghost stared back at her.

"I have tried to reconstruct it in my mind. It is so difficult. I can hear the shots. It may have been two or three, I don't know. Then Sam and I both reached for the kids. I was trying to pull them under the table, but she was clinging to them. Then there was lots of shots in sequence. Like a string of firecrackers going off. I think I heard a window shatter. Then the door burst open and this man came in. He was big and he was wearing a balaclava, and he started spraying the table, recklessly. It was terrifying. Everything was jumping and shattering."

I asked her, "What happened next?"

"Almost immediately Isileli burst in. he grabbed the man and they started wrestling. He screamed at me to go upstairs. I didn't want to leave the children. I was lying on top of them. I remember he grabbed me by my hair and dragged me to my feet—"

Gallin interrupted her. "What was the gunman doing while he did that?"

"I don't know. I think he had knocked him down. But he threw me out of the room, yelling at me to go upstairs. I tried to go back into the dining room, but the door burst open and the gunman came out. I ran." She stopped dead, staring at me with wide eyes. "I am ashamed. I ran. And he was right behind me. I could hear his boots on the stairs. I ran to my room and hid in the wardrobe, curled up on the floor." She paused again and closed her eyes. "And then there was this horrific noise of hammering on the door, glass shattering, wood splintering. I could feel the bullets passing over my head and smashing into the wall. I really thought I was going to die. Then it stopped suddenly and I just lay there, trembling, until the policeman opened the door. I thought he was going to shoot me."

I nodded. Gallin glanced at me. I said, "Senator. The assassin who had the list is dead."

She frowned at me. "I don't understand."

"He set a trap for me this evening. He believed he had killed Priti Anand and de Jong and Costello, and I was the next on his list."

"He believed...?"

I nodded. "The media cooperated with us. So that left only me on the list. He called pretending to be a Russian agent called Peter Belov, and said he wanted to meet. I went, prepared for it to be a trap, and I managed to kill the assassin."

"My god..." she said quietly. "But...," she screwed up her forehead, "but when was that?"

"About nine thirty PM. He was very small, slight, pale."

"But then who...?"

"Isileli Manu."

"No—"

"His real name is Isaiah Luomo, from the Island of Tonga. Wanted for murder and possession of class B drugs with intent to distribute. Escaped while on bail."

"No, that's not possible."

"When he killed Dolly, she scratched his arm and we got enough organic material to make a DNA profile." I pulled his handkerchief from my pocket. "And there is more than enough to make a comparison here." I slipped the handkerchief back. "He's an emotional guy."

"But I saw..."

I interrupted her. "It didn't make sense to me from the start that your name was underscored twice, but he went first for Paul, a close friend of yours, and then instead of taking you out next, he went all the way to LA to kill Senator Reed. Then it dawned on me that this was a punishment list, of people who had failed the Russians during the suitcase bombings. And when I realized that, I also realized that you were the only person on the list the Russians had no reason to punish."

Gallin blinked and turned to stare at me. I ignored her and held Troy's eye. She said nothing. So I went on, shaking my head, "The underscoring didn't mean you were a prime target," I laughed, "it meant it was your copy of the list! And *that* was why you sent Isileli to kill Dolly. By coming here I had unwittingly implicated her. You knew that the only way I could have got the list was from her."

She gazed down at her hands. "It's absurd. Why would I want to punish people on behalf of the Russians? You know what a strong influence Paul was on me. That would have been totally contrary to—"

I cut her short. "You have never followed Colonel Hirschfield's politics. Your politics have always been pragmatic at best, spineless at worst. You have always sought power and influence, and you have been willing to sell out wherever necessary to gain a powerful friend or an ally. You phoned Colonel Hirschfield the day he died to give him one last chance to back you. He was no fool, something in what you said to him, his knowledge of you, your relationship with Jerry—something in all that alerted him that he had just been given his last chance, and he sat to wait for your assassin with his P226 in his lap."

"You said it was a punishment list. Now you're saying—"

I cut her short again. "It was a punishment list for the Russians, which you facilitated through Jerry in exchange for them promoting your career. They eliminate the competition: Costello and Reed, Anand and de Jong, and you give them Hirschfield and me and promise, if they make you president, to sell them your country, just like you sold your friends and even your children."

"You must be out of your mind. Nobody will ever believe that."

"You needed to make the cops and ODIN believe that you were on that list as a victim. As far as you were aware, your little freak was coming to the end of his task, and we were going to be asking how come he never came after you? So you had to stage an attempt on your life, one that would be utterly convincing. You weren't about to have Isileli shoot you, you wanted to be in a fit state to capitalize on all the positive publicity, but what could be more convincing than to have him massacre your family? You who had already lost so much, and yet were still fighting on for the good of your country."

"You can't prove that. You can never prove that."

Outside, right on cue, a siren blasted twice. There were a couple of shouts. I rose and went to the window and looked down to where six cops were having a hard time wrestling Isaiah Luomo, AKA Isileli Manu, to the ground.

I made a doubtful face. "I don't know what to tell you,

Helen, I think with the right kind of motivation Mr. Luomo might become very talkative." Then I turned to face her. "And I am pretty sure, even though I would personally oppose it, there are people in the administration who might ease your sentence, if you were willing to name names here in Washington and also in Moscow." I shrugged. "You sacrificed your country, your friends and your children. Why not your employer?"

She didn't say anything for a moment. Then she said, "I'll need to see a proposal from the Attorney General, and discuss it with my lawyers."

"Sure. You can do all that from a secure location of ODIN's choosing. On your feet, Helen. You are under arrest."

EPILOGUE

"You knew."

"I suspected."

She had her feet on my lap in my backyard. The barbeque embers were dying down, exuding a lazy infernal glow, the aftermath of a very carnal dinner was littered on the table and we were sitting in a porch swing which I had in my backyard instead of my porch, finishing the wine.

"You should have told me."

I shook my head and sipped. "If I had you would have got all pushy and started saying it was an Israeli investigation and you were in charge and yadda yadda yadda."

"Yadda yadda yadda?"

"Mm-hmm. You are very disobedient."

"Disobedient. You know I'm going to shove this glass right up where the sun don't shine, right?"

"I told you, stay on Troy…"

"And you know what would have happened if I had, right? We'd be applying for special passes from Jewish

Heaven to Atheist Purgatory just so we could have dinner together. Because we would both be dead."

I made a 'Hmmm...' noise and sipped my wine. "We are practically there already. We inhabit different continents. You have to come to New York or Washington, or I have to go to London or Tel Aviv."

"So what?"

"What do you mean, so what?"

"We're friends. Friends visit each other. It's what friends do."

"You're a pain in the ass."

"What were you saying on the steps?"

"I was saying you're a pain in the ass. My wine is finished. We should move on to whiskey."

"Tell me."

"No. I was saying you're a pain in the ass."

She shook her head and giggled like a kid. "No, it sounded like, *Ah blub nyosh bulbj josh ha*." She threw back her head and laughed. Then she imitated me, hunching her shoulders like she was carrying a heavy load, *"Ah blub nyosh bulbj josh ha!"* Suddenly she became serious. "I heard some of it, Mason."

"Oh, Jesus."

"You were kind of slobbering and kept calling me baby, or *blehbleh*. And you told me you were not going to leave me there."

"Yeah, well, you know, curare will do that to a guy, before it kills him. Are we done?"

There was a lot of warmth in her eyes and in her slow smile. "I don't know. I'm in no hurry. But I think you should go get that Bushmills."

Don't miss DEAD MAN TALKING. The riveting sequel in the Alex Mason Thriller series.

Scan the QR code below to purchase DEAD MAN TALKING.

Or go to: righthouse.com/dead-man-talking

NOTE: flip to the very end to read an exclusive sneak peak...

DON'T MISS ANYTHING!

If you want to stay up to date on all new releases in this series, with these authors, or with any of our new deals, you can do so by joining our newsletters below.

In addition, you will immediately gain access to our entire *Right House VIP Library,* which currently includes *ORIGINS*—a full length prequel novel to *ODIN.*

righthouse.com/email

(Easy to unsubscribe. No spam. Ever.)

ALSO BY DAVID ARCHER

Up to date books can be found at:
www.righthouse.com/david-archer

ROGUE THRILLERS
Gates of Hell (Book 1)
Hell's Fury (Book 2)

JACOB HUNTER THRILLERS
The Kyiv File (Book 1)
The Bogota File (Book 2)

PETER BLACK THRILLERS
Burden of the Assassin (Book 1)
The Man Without A Face (Book 2)
Unpunished Deeds (Book 3)
Hunter Killer (Book 4)
Silent Shadows (Book 5)
The Last Run (Book 6)
Dark Corners (Book 7)
Ghost Operative (Book 8)

ALEX MASON THRILLERS
Odin (Book 1)
Ice Cold Spy (Book 2)
Mason's Law (Book 3)
Assets and Liabilities (Book 4)
Russian Roulette (Book 5)

Executive Order (Book 6)
Dead Man Talking (Book 7)
All The King's Men (Book 8)
Flashpoint (Book 9)
Brotherhood of the Goat (Book 10)
Dead Hot (Book 11)
Blood on Megiddo (Book 12)
Son of Hell (Book 13)

NOAH WOLF THRILLERS

Code Name Camelot (Book 1)
Lone Wolf (Book 2)
In Sheep's Clothing (Book 3)
Hit for Hire (Book 4)
The Wolf's Bite (Book 5)
Black Sheep (Book 6)
Balance of Power (Book 7)
Time to Hunt (Book 8)
Red Square (Book 9)
Highest Order (Book 10)
Edge of Anarchy (Book 11)
Unknown Evil (Book 12)
Black Harvest (Book 13)
World Order (Book 14)
Caged Animal (Book 15)
Deep Allegiance (Book 16)
Pack Leader (Book 17)
High Treason (Book 18)
A Wolf Among Men (Book 19)
Rogue Intelligence (Book 20)
Alpha (Book 21)

Rogue Wolf (Book 22)
Shadows of Allegiance (Book 23)
In the Grip of Darkness (Book 24)

SAM PRICHARD MYSTERIES
The Grave Man (Book 1)
Death Sung Softly (Book 2)
Love and War (Book 3)
Framed (Book 4)
The Kill List (Book 5)
Drifter: Part One (Book 6)
Drifter: Part Two (Book 7)
Drifter: Part Three (Book 8)
The Last Song (Book 9)
Ghost (Book 10)
Hidden Agenda (Book 11)

SAM AND INDIE MYSTERIES
Aces and Eights (Book 1)
Fact or Fiction (Book 2)
Close to Home (Book 3)
Brave New World (Book 4)
Innocent Conspiracy (Book 5)
Unfinished Business (Book 6)
Live Bait (Book 7)
Alter Ego (Book 8)
More Than It Seems (Book 9)
Moving On (Book 10)
Worst Nightmare (Book 11)
Chasing Ghosts (Book 12)
Serial Superstition (Book 13)

CHANCE REDDICK THRILLERS
Innocent Injustice (Book 1)
Angel of Justice (Book 2)
High Stakes Hunting (Book 3)
Personal Asset (Book 4)

CASSIE MCGRAW MYSTERIES
What Lies Beneath (Book 1)
Can't Fight Fate (Book 2)
One Last Game (Book 3)
Never Really Gone (Book 4)

ALSO BY BLAKE BANNER

Up to date books can be found at:
www.righthouse.com/blake-banner

ROGUE THRILLERS
Gates of Hell (Book 1)
Hell's Fury (Book 2)

ALEX MASON THRILLERS
Odin (Book 1)
Ice Cold Spy (Book 2)
Mason's Law (Book 3)
Assets and Liabilities (Book 4)
Russian Roulette (Book 5)
Executive Order (Book 6)
Dead Man Talking (Book 7)
All The King's Men (Book 8)
Flashpoint (Book 9)
Brotherhood of the Goat (Book 10)
Dead Hot (Book 11)
Blood on Megiddo (Book 12)
Son of Hell (Book 13)

HARRY BAUER THRILLER SERIES
Dead of Night (Book 1)
Dying Breath (Book 2)
The Einstaat Brief (Book 3)

Quantum Kill (Book 4)
Immortal Hate (Book 5)
The Silent Blade (Book 6)
LA: Wild Justice (Book 7)
Breath of Hell (Book 8)
Invisible Evil (Book 9)
The Shadow of Ukupacha (Book 10)
Sweet Razor Cut (Book 11)
Blood of the Innocent (Book 12)
Blood on Balthazar (Book 13)
Simple Kill (Book 14)
Riding The Devil (Book 15)
The Unavenged (Book 16)
The Devil's Vengeance (Book 17)
Bloody Retribution (Book 18)
Rogue Kill (Book 19)
Blood for Blood (Book 20)

DEAD COLD MYSTERY SERIES
An Ace and a Pair (Book 1)
Two Bare Arms (Book 2)
Garden of the Damned (Book 3)
Let Us Prey (Book 4)
The Sins of the Father (Book 5)
Strange and Sinister Path (Book 6)
The Heart to Kill (Book 7)
Unnatural Murder (Book 8)
Fire from Heaven (Book 9)
To Kill Upon A Kiss (Book 10)
Murder Most Scottish (Book 11)

The Butcher of Whitechapel (Book 12)
Little Dead Riding Hood (Book 13)
Trick or Treat (Book 14)
Blood Into Wine (Book 15)
Jack In The Box (Book 16)
The Fall Moon (Book 17)
Blood In Babylon (Book 18)
Death In Dexter (Book 19)
Mustang Sally (Book 20)
A Christmas Killing (Book 21)
Mommy's Little Killer (Book 22)
Bleed Out (Book 23)
Dead and Buried (Book 24)
In Hot Blood (Book 25)
Fallen Angels (Book 26)
Knife Edge (Book 27)
Along Came A Spider (Book 28)
Cold Blood (Book 29)
Curtain Call (Book 30)

THE OMEGA SERIES
Dawn of the Hunter (Book 1)
Double Edged Blade (Book 2)
The Storm (Book 3)
The Hand of War (Book 4)
A Harvest of Blood (Book 5)
To Rule in Hell (Book 6)
Kill: One (Book 7)
Powder Burn (Book 8)
Kill: Two (Book 9)
Unleashed (Book 10)

The Omicron Kill (Book 11)
9mm Justice (Book 12)
Kill: Four (Book 13)
Death In Freedom (Book 14)
Endgame (Book 15)

ABOUT US

Right House is an independent publisher created by authors for readers. We specialize in Action, Thriller, Mystery, and Crime novels.

If you enjoyed this novel, then there is a good chance you will like what else we have to offer! Please stay up to date by using any of the links below.

Join our mailing lists to stay up to date -->
righthouse.com/email
Visit our website --> righthouse.com
Contact us --> contact@righthouse.com

facebook.com/righthousebooks
x.com/righthousebooks
instagram.com/righthousebooks

EXCLUSIVE SNEAK PEAK OF...

DEAD MAN TALKING

PROLOGUE

THE DOORBELL RANG AND SAUL SIGHED. SAUL sighed a lot these days. He paused a moment before standing, to look out the open French doors at the glimmering lights of the wet city, five floors below. The wrought iron of the small balcony framed the streetlamps of Church Street. They were glimmering, he thought, not glittering. Glittering was too sparkly. That was New York, Los Angeles, even San Francisco. These lights were softer, wetter, more mellow, like the city. His city. A small smile, as mellow as the lights, touched his eyes. He knew that many thought of him as a traitor, especially in the liberal community, and of his city as a den of corruption and savagery. He didn't accept either. He had betrayed no one, and as for corruption, that was what "They" had done to it. To him this was the home—the source—of everything good and decent and right about humanity.

The doorbell rang again and he sighed again, forced himself to his feet, groaning with middle age, and with his hands on the small of his back, he walked stretching from his cluttered, comfortable office, across his spacious living room to his front door, and opened it.

He frowned and sagged slightly. "I am real busy. This is not a good time."

On receiving no response he turned and walked away from the door, talking over his shoulder as he went. "Fine! Come on in then, but please, make it brief. I lose my thread when I'm distracted..."

He heard the door close softly. Then, "Saul...?" Something in the voice made him stop and turn. He got as far as, "What...?" before the .44 caliber slug punched a half-inch hole into his forehead and a four-inch hole out the back of his head, spraying his considerable brains across the parquet floor and the genuine Persian rug. He went down straight like a tree and hit the floor with a jarring smack.

His visitor smiled. "You always complained of a stiff back. I bet it's never been as stiff as this, has it?"

His visitor then crossed the living room to Saul's study.

CHAPTER 1

It was raining on Campden Hill Square. It was not so much heavy as steady, relentless. You got the feeling it could go on like this indefinitely, till long after you had become exhausted and died of old age. There was the steady sound of wet splatter—an overflowing gutter somewhere—and through the open window of my rented Jaguar I could smell damp wooden fenceposts and creosote. It was a very English smell on a very English day and I loved it.

The blacktop was slick and shiny, and the early afternoon lights lay in liquid trails in the thin film of water. The streets were empty and, freed from human observers, the oaks, sycamores and chestnut trees in the garden at the center of the square were all nodding sagely to each other, like they were deep in Entish dialogue.

I hadn't seen Gallin since she'd been assigned to work with me on the Helen Troy execution list in DC.[1] She had gone back to London, I had spent time convalescing, and we had kind of lost touch. Now I could see warm light in her living-room window and wondered if I should go and knock on the door. The moment's hesitation was resolved when the door opened and she stepped out with her collar turned up and an Irish, Donegal tweed cap on her head. She hunched her shoulders but didn't hurry. She trotted down the steps from her front lawn, glanced at me and came and opened the passenger door.

"Nice car!"

I smiled. "Hello stranger. Get in and you won't get wet."

She climbed in, slammed the door and removed her hat. Her hair was tied in a knot behind her head and now she untied it, retied it and tightened it as she spoke.

"It's been a long time. Months. What happened? Battery ran out on your phone?"

"Straight in, huh?" I smiled at her but she pretended to be busy with her hair. I shrugged and pulled away from the curb. At Notting Hill Gate I said, "I got the impression you were busy."

"I was," she said with something in her mouth. She took the something out and put it in her hair. "But I wasn't too busy to talk."

I shrugged again. It was a shrugging kind of conversation. "That wasn't the impression I got. You didn't call either."

"Well, ain't we like a couple of fifteen-year-old kids!"

"You know what Richard Bandler said—"

"He's back, Mr. Erudite Quotes. Bandler said a lot of things. That guy never shuts up. You hear his story about the guy who went to hospital with a ferret up his ass?" I looked at her. She said, "Sorry. What did he say, Alex?"

"Communication is always what the other person understands."

"Oh, that's very good. So, if to me 'kick you in the nuts' means 'have your babies' and I say to you, 'Alex, I want to have your babies,' but you understand, 'Alex, I want to kick you in the nuts,' that is what I have actually communicated?"

We had reached Marble Arch and I turned down Park Lane. The traffic there is like an intersection between the nine levels of hell. So I didn't answer until I'd turned left into Mount Street, left again into Park Street, cruised up among elegant, rain-washed Georgian buildings until as far as number thirty-seven (a grand, massive gray stone edifice five stories high, with great bay windows and elegant arches), and stopped the car. Then I looked at her.

"Yes, it is always wise to make sure we communicate what we want the other person to understand, rather than expect them to read our minds. Shall we go up?"

"Yeah," she said. "Let's go up."

The lobby was small, with a stone flagged floor and an old-fashioned elevator with a concertina door. I fitted a key I had been given by Nero to the panel where the buttons were, turned it, and the elevator carried us, squeaking and rattling, to a sixth floor the building appeared not to have. Gallin stared at me all the way. When the elevator had shuddered to a halt, she kept staring as she pulled back the concertina and we stepped out into a corridor of gray stone with a thread-bare red carpet. At the end there was a large, oak door with a brass knob in the center.

I rang the bell and it was opened almost immediately by

a tall, angular woman in a knee-length gray skirt and a white blouse. She bent her knees slightly and smiled.

"Yes?" Her voice bordered on the shrill.

"I'm Alex Mason, this is Captain Aila Gallin."

She looked delighted, "Oh, *yes!*" she said. "*Do* come in. You don't mind if we just go through the steps." She closed the door and led us to what appeared to be a three-in-one printer on her desk, but turned out not to be. "Hand on there, look in here, don't move." We were scanned and processed and she gave a little clap. "There we are, all done! Super! Through that door over there, Sir John will see you straight away."

A door beside her desk opened and admitted us to another long, gray stone corridor. Halfway down on the left there was a door. A young man in a suit stepped out and grinned.

"Mr. Mason? Captain Gallin? How do you do? I am Nigel, Sir John's secretary. Please, this way, Sir John is expecting you." We followed him in to a small, cramped antechamber with a desk, a filing cabinet and a tray. "Can I bring you tea? Coffee?"

We declined and he opened yet another door into a very large, very comfortable office with a burgundy carpet, oak panels and glass-fronted bookcases. Sir John rose from a desk you could play billiards on, which he had positioned in a vast bay with tall Georgian windows behind him.

He was tall and had that peculiar, understated English elegance that you can only get by going to Winchester Boys' School and then Oxford.

"Captain Gallin, what a pleasure to meet you at last.

Your father and I are old friends. And Mr. Mason, Nero speaks very highly of you," his smile became humorous, "though I daresay he never lets on. Please, do sit."

We sat in red leather chairs and he sat across from us. He frowned and tapped his desk a few times with his pencil.

"Has Nero given you any idea what this is about?"

I shook my head. "No, not at all. All I know is that he has taken the unusual step of asking the Mossad to second Captain Gallin to us..."

"Yes, that was our request. I am in the UK branch of ODIN, you understand. What Nero is in the United States, I am here. When we had a look at the case, we thought it might be of interest to Israel."

I smiled pleasantly, feeling myself getting antsy. I was barely two hours off the plane and sorely in need of a couple of martinis and a primal steak. "What case?"

"Quite so, let me start at the beginning." He stood and walked to a dresser he had against one wall. There he poured three tumblers of whisky as he spoke.

"I am quite certain you have heard of Saul Epstein—"

I turned in my chair. "The TV show host? Investigative journalist. Specializes in big exposés."

"That's the chap. American, originally from Boston, though his parents were originally from Kent. Brilliant fellow, Harvard *and* Oxford, degree in history and doctoral thesis on the roots of social liberty in society. Bit of an Anglophile. Good read.

"Worked as a reporter on the *New York Times*, though he found their ethos uncongenial, then editor of the *Herald Tribune*, then moved to television production, anchor on nationally syndicated morning news and finally got his own show. What most people didn't realize was that he had settled in London some ten years ago and he used to shuttle back and forth to New York."

He carried over the glasses and set them on the desk. As he sat, I said, "Forgive me, Sir John, but—" I hesitated a moment, trying to find a diplomatic way of asking the question. "How does this affect ODIN?"

His eyebrows rose as he sipped. "Oh, well, he's dead."

"Oh—"

"Murdered."

"Oh, but I still don't see..."

"He was found by the janitor in his apartment on Kensington Church Street. ten PM, last Friday, 9th September."

I frowned and shrugged one shoulder. "It's a police matter."

His smile was thin, amiable and as friendly as a kick in the nuts. "If it were, Mr. Mason, I wouldn't have asked Nero to send his best man, and asked Gabriel Gallin to second us his best officer in London."

I returned him an equally thin smile. "I imagine you wouldn't, Sir John. What I meant to say was, what is it about this murder that makes it of interest to ODIN?"

"Allow me to tell you."

Gallin turned to me with a smile that was thinner than both of ours and said, "What Sir John is saying, Alex, is shut up and let him finish."

Sir John chuckled but didn't deny it.

"In recent years Saul had become increasingly...," he paused a moment, "I don't want to say obsessed, because that implies it was somehow irrational, and Saul was anything but irrational. But he had become extremely concerned with..."

Gallin sat forward, "Excuse me, Sir John." He looked at her with raised eyebrows. "You said, 'Saul'—you were on first-name terms?"

Again the thin smile. "We were close friends. Do you think that's relevant, Captain?"

"I don't know. And that's where I am going to file it."

"Splendid. So, he had become extremely concerned with what he saw as the overpopulation of the planet, nano-technology and genetic engineering. I asked him several times to clarify his concerns for me, but he refused. His precise words, the last time we spoke, were, 'When my research is finished, you'll be the first to read it.'"

Gallin spoke again, "What connects those three fields of research is that all three are concerned with very large numbers of people."

"Precisely."

"That and one other related point," I added. "Power. Power over not large, but immense sections of the population. Nano-technology applied to genetic engineering is a nightmare scenario from which we are separated by tissue paper."

"That is how Saul saw it. He said we could be looking at the fazing out of humanity over the next century or two. He said we had become redundant to ourselves."

"Visionaries." Gallin snorted. "In the past visionaries were dangerous because they started wars. Today visionaries have access to the technology to upgrade humanity, and terminate the race in the process. Yesterday's visionaries are today's messiahs and angels of death."

He nodded at his desk for a moment. "Some might accuse you of overstating the case, Captain Gallin, but I think you are right on the money. Saul would certainly have agreed with you. Today they are celebrities."

I said, "You think he was murdered because of his research." It wasn't a question. It was a conclusion.

"It seems likely. Saul was a popular man. He had very few enemies."

Gallin, quick as a viper, was in there. "Few..."

He shook his head sadly and took a sip of whisky. "Saul was not what you'd call handsome. But, from what I am told that is not necessarily a primary consideration with women." He glanced apologetically at Gallin. "Of course one has to be very careful with that kind of statement these days, one never knows what might be construed as offensive or misogynistic. However, in Saul's case, women seemed to be fascinated by him, despite his looks, and a physical condition which was, shall we say, marred by good living. He had been married three times. He was on reasonably good terms with his last wife, Julia, but he'd had a string of affairs. The last of these, Naomi Gordon, became very upset when she discovered that he had been having meetings with his ex-wife."

Gallin said, "Naomi Gordon? The model?"

"Yes, she's actually a highly intelligent woman, but venomously jealous. You know her, Mr. Mason?"

I shook my head. "Should I?"

Sir John cleared his throat. "Well, I mean, she is quite spectacular, really,"

Gallin cut him short. "Six-foot-one, black, but I mean *real* black, not Latina with a suntan, we are talking *ebony*. Built like a goddess, aquiline nose and almond eyes the size of small vases."

"Small vases?"

"Yeah, I couldn't think of anything almond shaped. All the way up legs. She was voted the most beautiful woman in the world by *Vogue* magazine or something." She turned a skeptical face to Sir John. "I didn't realize she had a brain though. Women that beautiful usually have brains like sparrow shit."

Sir John suppressed a laugh. "Yes, well, in her case she got a first in history from the LSE. Which," he then said "which" three times very quickly, "Which, which, which... *these* days does not perhaps mean as much as it might have done some years ago, but still. She is definitely an intelligent woman."

I said, "And she had it out for Saul Epstein because he had been seeing his ex-wife?"

"Yes. Julia, of course, is *extremely* intelligent. First class degree from Oxford in the classics—that was back in the 1980s, of course, when Oxford was still a good university. She then wrote her doctoral thesis on the subject of totalitarian societies, arguing that society pulls simultaneously, equally and irresistibly toward totalitarianism and anarchy, making a state of constant conflict inescapable. Saul found her fascinating. He often said that a good intellect was far more sexually arousing than a beautiful body. He was, he said, sapiosexual."

"Why'd they split up?"

"She left him. As well as sapiosexual, he was also plain

heterosexual and she found his philandering insulting, and in the end I think she found him a trifle childish."

Gallin scratched her head under her Irish tweed cap and made the face of skepticism. "You think Naomi Gordon was that crazy about him she'd kill him out of jealousy? I mean, she could have pretty much any man she wanted."

Sir John drew breath but I answered for him.

"That's not quite right, Gallin. In the first place, a lot of modern men feel intimidated by a woman like Naomi Gordon. Speaking purely sexually, a man needs a lot of vitality to satisfy a woman as intense as that. Most modern men, raised on a diet of fast food and vegan guilt, don't feel up to the job. If she is intelligent too, for every man she attracts, she is scaring off ten."

Gallin rolled her eyes. I ignored her and went on. "On the other hand, she doesn't need to be in love with Saul to feel rage. If her trophy man is having private meetings with his brilliant ex-wife, and that gets reported on social media, the humiliation for her would be huge. That would be enough to drive a narcissist to murder."

Sir John was nodding vigorously. "I agree with you one hundred and ten percent, on the...umm...second point. But equally I am certain that this was not what happened. Our concern—and let us pray that we are wrong—is that that he was assassinated because of the research he was doing, and that the research had to do with genetic engineering, over-population, and nano-technology."

"You have any leads? Any place we can start?"

He shook his head and stared at me for a moment. "That's why I asked Nero for you, and Gabriel for Captain Gallin. It is also one of the things that makes me quite certain it was an assassination. If Naomi had killed him, there would have been a frightful mess. But there is nothing, absolutely nothing, at the scene of the crime to indicate a crime has been committed, except the body. It takes a very good professional to do that."

I nodded a few times and Gallin nodded once and added, "It does."

CHAPTER 2

Sir John had dropped a very thin manila file on his desk and told us that was what there was of the police report. "We killed the police investigation as soon as we heard, but I shouldn't think they'd have got much further than they did anyway."

Inside, it contained the keys to Epstein's apartment, a couple of sheets of printed paper and a second envelope full of photographs.

After that he'd told us, "You may need to go beyond what is strictly legal, so we would be grateful if you would contact us as little as possible to ensure credible deniability. As you know, the Office of the Director of Information Networks requires the utmost secrecy."

"Your deniability is safe with us," I'd told him, and we left. On the way down in the 19th-century concertina elevator I had told Gallin, "You drive, I want to get carsick reading the report."

Now we were in the car weaving and battling through

traffic that did not benefit from the grid system because most of the winding, bending roads, streets, crescents, places, passages, ends, walks and mews were probably originally cattle tracks that dated back to the Neolithic age.

"Where are we going?" I asked as I tried to read.

"Well, Alex, I thought it might be a good idea to go and have a chat with Julia, his ex-wife. Ask me why. I promise you won't be encroaching on my privacy, my space or my work."

I took a deep breath and tried not to sigh.

"Why, Aila?"

"Well, for a start, she is apparently a highly intelligent woman, first class degree in the classics from Oxford—back in the 1980s when Oxford was still a good university— doctoral thesis in anthropology—plus, Saul found her so fascinating he couldn't keep his dirty little sapiosexual hands off her, despite the risk of being rejected." She gave me a look, like she had a meat grinder in her hands and was about to drop my testicles in it. "Jewish men are like that sometimes. We call them mensch. Or sometimes just, you know... men. A guy with balls who won't take no for an answer."

"Can we stay on task, Gallin."

I would have got more response from my late great-grandmother.

"A woman likes that sometimes. Shows a guy cares and is prepared to fight for what he wants. He calls: 'I need to see you, let's have dinner.' 'I can't. I'm busy.' 'Busy how? Make time.' 'I can't make time, Saul, I have a deadline!' 'Tell them you'll be late. I'm coming over. Wear something nice.'"

"Are you done?"

"Yes, Alex, my point is, she fascinated him, and being the

kind of *man* he was, there was none of this limp-wristed, 'I don't want to intrude, I respect your space' crap. So they must have been pretty close and *intimate*."

"So she might know something. OK, it's a good place to start."

"Yes, Alex."

We drove west along Kensington High Street, with the immensely green park on our right and huge, red busses all around us, till we came to Victoria Road. There we turned left among elegant Victorian mansions on the right and a grotesque monument to the Hive on the left. A short drive down we turned into Albert Place, a short, elegant street with more trees than houses. What houses there were had that solid elegance of the early decades of the 20th century. They were painted white or cream, with gray slate roofs, and were all partially hidden behind an abundance of foliage.

We pulled up outside a well-trimmed hedge and Gallin killed the engine. The windshield wipers gave two dying squeaks and stopped. Raindrops began to accumulate on the glass.

"Shall we go?"

She gave me a once-over with her eyes, nodded and got out.

By the time I'd got to the gate she had climbed the seven steps to the porch and was ringing on the brass bell beside the dark, glossy blue door. There was a rich smell of damp earth and autumn leaves on the air. The door opened as I came up beside her. There was a middle-aged woman holding the door and looking at us like we might be the next bad thing that was going to happen that day. She didn't say anything. She just clenched her fists and held them to her chest.

Gallin spoke first, "We are here to see Mrs. Epstein. Is she in?"

Her reply came in what the Brits call cut-glass English. It was also shrill and nasal. "She's indisposed. You'll have to go away and come back at another time!"

Gallin smiled and nodded. She had the same cut-glass English, only it wasn't shrill or nasal. "I'm sure she is. We are attached to Whitehall and we need to ask her some questions."

"No. I'm sorry. It's out of the question! Whitehall, you say?" She shook her head quickly. "No, sorry, makes no difference."

"The only problem is, if we go away and come back with a warrant, we'll have to bring police cars with sirens and it all gets very embarrassing."

The woman's jaw dropped. "That's outrageous!"

I nodded. "And noisy," I said. "It's very regrettable. Perhaps the simplest thing..." I shrugged and smiled.

She lifted her chin. "I shall go and speak to Mrs. Epstein. She may want to call her solicitor!"

"I hope not," I said with the nicest smile I had. "We really want to keep this discreet. The last thing the government wants is a media circus."

Her eyes went wide, she turned on her heel and marched away. She came back within a couple of minutes and spoke with cruel severity.

"You may come in! But *please*, be brief, and then leave!"

She led us past tasteful hunting prints to a spacious, elegant drawing room which was the more elegant for being slightly disordered and clearly enjoyed and lived it. There was a Georgian fireplace with a brass fireguard in front of it and a huge, pale gray calico sofa backing onto open French windows. Outside a lawn was turning slowly into a marsh and a metal barbeque was turning to rust. The only light was from the open windows, so half the room—the half with the armchairs in it—was in shadow.

Lying on the sofa was a woman in her sixties. Her hair had been a wild red, but was now streaked with occasional silver. She watched us with eyes that had learned to be ironic instead of bitter. You could read the intelligence in her face, and I could see why Saul had found her so attractive.

"A media circus? Seriously? Low, cheap blackmail." I was surprised to hear her accent was American. "I've let you in because I want Saul's killer caught, not because I am giving in to your threats. Who are you?"

Gallin showed her a fake ID she had apparently been supplied with, which said she was with Military Intelligence Section 5, and I showed her a plastic card that said I was with the Pentagon's Office of the Director of Intelligence which was true in an abstract sense; like Picasso's people with both eyes on the same side of their face.

She scrutinized both with interest and handed them back. "Neither of you is a cop. And you," she said, pointing at me, "you're from Washington. What's going on?"

I smiled again. I was doing a lot of smiling that morning, mainly at people who didn't appreciate it. "I *am* from Washington, Mrs. Epstein, and as you can probably tell this is a little complicated. I'd hate you to get a crick in your neck while we explain."

"Sit down, Alex Mason, and you'd better sit too,

Captain. I am extremely upset, so I hope you're not going to tax me. Why is Saul's death being investigated by spies instead of cops?"

Gallin snorted a small laugh. "That's pretty much what we hoped you would tell us."

Julia Epstein narrowed her eyes. "Run that by me again, sweet cheeks."

"Whitehall has asked us to look into your husband's—"

"Ex-husband—"

"Ex-husband's death because they believe there may be a political motive to the murder."

"As opposed to the more common motives of sex and money?"

Gallin nodded.

Julia shrugged and pulled down the corners of her mouth. "I guess the only person with any real motive to kill Saul for ordinary human reasons was me. He used to drive me mad. But every time I thought about shooting the bastard, I remembered how much I loved him."

Her lip curled in and she started to cry, without embarrassment or hysterics, looking down at a handkerchief she kept folding and unfolding. "I am really going to miss him. I miss him already."

"What about Naomi Gordon?" I asked.

"No." She shook her head. "You need strength of character to kill somebody. Either that or provocation beyond endurance. You know one, surefire way to tell whether someone has strength of character?"

"Tell me."

"If they are gifted with intelligence, and they make nothing of value out of their lives. Get a good degree! Write a book! Discover something! Help people! Make your life valuable somehow! But get rich by showing the world what a great body you've got?" She leaned forward, turning from me to Gallin as she spoke. "*Why the hell isn't that girl frustrated out of her mind? I'll tell you.*" She sank back into the sofa again. "Because she is a narcissist, with no ambition, and no strength of character. She would not kill Saul. She *could* not kill Saul. The best she could do in the way of punishing him would be to have herself photographed with as many beautiful, sexually ambiguous men as possible, with her mouth wide open in a mindless grin, post them on her social media pages or whatever the hell they are, and hope that he'd feel jealous. That's it. Virtual revenge through virtual pain."

Gallin stepped in and pulled us back on track.

"We understand you had a pretty tight friendship, and Mr. Epstein confided in you."

"That's true up to a point. I was probably the only person in the world Saul actually loved. He was a selfish, domineering bastard with no time for weak people. At the same time, he was noble. He was on a crusade to expose the sons of bitches who exploit, denigrate and abuse humanity. It sounds contradictory, but he used to say he was with Snoopy. He loved mankind, it was people he couldn't stand. So, if he shared any details of his research or investigation with anyone, it would be me." She shook her head. "But he hardly ever mentioned any details about his investigations."

Gallin leaned forward. Her eyes were intense. "I don't want to pressure you, Mrs. Epstein, but you may be the only person who has any clue at all as to who murdered Saul, and why. Is there anything, however trivial, you can think of that might help us to know what he was working on? Any passing comments, names he mentioned, people he'd been in touch with..."

"Back in the day he was friends with William Rees-Mogg. Rees-Mogg was an intellectual, a lateral thinker, politically involved and totally radical, a fascinating guy. He talked to Saul about nano-technology and how it was going to change society. That made an impact on Saul and he became more and more obsessed with it as the technology advanced. And in the last two or three years, that was all he would talk about, nano-technology, genetic engineering *using* nano-technology, and what he called 'the darkness' that was enveloping the planet. The new Dark Age."

Gallin frowned. "What did he mean by that?"

"According to Saul, humanity is a plague. Trouble is, we are also at the top of the food chain. And according to him that meant that we would be driven, by nature itself, to destroy ourselves. The more we swarmed over the globe, the more self-destructive our behavior would become. And he particularly saw this in the elite. Those with absolute temporal power. The billionaire club—those who count their billions in tens and hundreds. He was increasingly convinced that they had an agenda to cull humanity—"

"Excuse me?" It was Gallin, frowning.

"You heard me right, honey—*cull*. That is the word he used. There are too many of us, and what do you do with a species when there are too many of them? You cull them."

"Forgive my saying so, Mrs. Epstein, but it sounds like the kind of science fiction conspiracy theory you find on the internet."

She laughed. "Oh, I forgive you and I agree with you. And that was what I told Saul, only not so nicely. And you know what he said? He looked at me and he said, 'Science fiction, Julia? Like Asimov and *Star Trek*? We left science fiction behind a long time ago.' He said, 'The technology to do what I am talking about already exists. All that is missing is the political will to do it.' And then he asked me, 'Or is it?'" She spread her hands, washing them of any involvement in Saul's crazy ideas. "Anyway, you asked me what he was working on. That's as much as I know about what he was working on."

I asked, "Did he give you any names of corporations or people?"

"Not that I can recall." She frowned, like she was having trouble understanding something. "I am very tired, and I'd like to be alone with my thoughts now. If I think of anything, I'll let you know."

I nodded. "Of course. I am really very sorry." I stood and took out my card. As I set it on the table beside her I said, "Just before we go, who were his close friends, his intimate circle?"

Her face became depressed. She gave her head a helpless little shake. "Me. People he had close contact with? Well, his producer, obviously, that's Pamela, Pamela Peach-Plum, and that playboy philanderer..." She thought for a moment. "... His lawyer, Nick, Nick Barnes. They were the only people he had close contact with. And Naomi, of course, but that was just sex. He had no respect for her as a person."

When we stepped outside, the rain had eased to a slight drizzle, but the eaves, guttering and upper floor windowsills were dripping in a wet, broken rhythm. Occasional cars passed nearby with a wet sigh. Everything was wet.

I descended the steps to the sidewalk with Gallin behind

me. I went to the passenger side and leaned on the roof, making my sleeves wet. She opened the driver's door and stopped, looking at me.

"What?"

I screwed up my face in thought. "Epstein's apartment. Then we need a pub with a fire and meat pies."

She nodded. "Sure." She climbed in and I got in next to her. "His apartment is just up the road, in Church Street."

We pulled away and turned up toward the High Street. She drove in silence. Finally I said, "We need to clear the air, Gallin. Or this is going to interfere with our work."

She held up two fingers in the V sign. "One, I have worked very efficiently many times with people I really did not like, in sullen silence, and we got the job done very efficiently. You don't need to get on well with someone to work well with them. Two, is that your main reason for wanting to clear the air? To make sure it does not prejudice the job?"

I rolled my eyes and asked the gods to give me patience.

"Yes, of course it is possible. No, that is not my main reason. Gallin, this is getting out of hand. We need to stop."

"Yup, and the longer you avoid it, the worse it's going to get. Alex, I am this far," she held up her thumb and forefinger and they were practically touching, *"this far*, from telling you to go to hell." I drew breath but she cut me short. "Tell me one more time that it is affecting our work and I *will* tell you to go to hell."

"OK, that was a poor choice of words—"

"And don't even *dream*," she said as we turned into Church Street, "of proving your feminist credentials to me by showing how sensitive you are and revealing your feminine side."

I drew breath again but she cut me short again. "You don't want to stay in touch? That's fine. You don't need to explain yourself to me. We just do the job and get it done. You go back to DC, I stay home in London. Sorted."

"OK, Gallin, you made your point! Now shut up and let me talk, will you?"

She slammed on the brakes and skidded to a halt by the curb. A car honked behind us and then passed with an angry glare. I stared at Gallin and she jerked her chin at my door. "Get out."

"*What?*"

"Get out! We're here. This is his apartment block."

She climbed out and made her way toward the building. I sat a moment swearing softly under my breath, then got out and went after her.

Scan the QR code below to purchase DEAD MAN TALKING.
Or go to: righthouse.com/dead-man-talking

NOTES

CHAPTER 1

1. See *Russian Roulette*
2. See *Russian Roulette*

CHAPTER 13

1. My Lady

CHAPTER 1

1. See *Executive Order*